AF226562

My Deranged Boss

Trapped in a toxic office under a delusional boss's reign of rage and fraud

Amanda Ray

My Deranged Boss

Copyright © 2026 Amanda Ray

All rights reserved. No part of this book may be reproduced, stored in a retrieval system, or transmitted in any form or by any means — electronic, mechanical, photocopying, recording, or otherwise — without the prior written permission of the author, except in the case of brief quotations embodied in critical reviews and certain other non-commercial uses permitted by copyright law.

This is a work of fiction. Names, characters, businesses, organisations, places, events, and incidents are either the product of the author's imagination or are used fictitiously. Any resemblance to actual persons, living or dead, or actual events is purely coincidental.

First published 2026

Printed in the United States of America

Paperback ISBN: 978-1-972750-00-1

Hardcover ISBN: 978-1-972750-01-8

*For everyone who ever smiled through gritted teeth
and documented everything. You know who you are.*

Table of Contents

Welcome to the Circus

I stepped into the RT Construction office on my first day with a mix of excitement and nerves buzzing in my stomach. After months of job hunting following my layoff, this felt like a fresh start. The building was a standard gray box in an industrial park, but the sign out front gleamed with promise: "RT Construction - Building the Future." I smoothed my blouse, adjusted my messenger bag, and pushed through the glass doors, ready to make a good impression.

The lobby was tidy, with framed photos of completed projects lining the walls—shiny new strip malls, sturdy bridges, and happy clients shaking hands with workers in hard hats. A receptionist desk sat empty, but voices drifted from the open-plan office beyond. The air smelled faintly of stale coffee and printer ink. It looked professional enough, like any small construction firm trying to punch above its weight. I took a deep breath and followed the signs to the admin area.

That's when I noticed the tension. It hung in the air like humidity before a storm, thick enough to cut with a knife. Phones rang unanswered, papers piled haphazardly on desks, and the few people visible moved with hurried, hunched shoulders. No one smiled or waved hello. My high hopes flickered just a bit.

"You must be the new office manager," a voice said from behind a computer screen. A woman in her late thirties popped up, her tight dark curls pulled into a no-nonsense bun. She had deep brown eyes that looked shadowed by exhaustion, like she hadn't slept in a week. Sturdy build, mom jeans, sensible blouse, she radiated quiet efficiency. "I'm Felicity Arden. Welcome to the circus."

I shook her hand, introducing myself as Emily Harris. "Nice to meet you. Circus? That doesn't sound promising."

Felicity gave a wry smile that didn't reach her eyes. "You'll see. Here's your desk; right next to the coffee machine that's been broken for two weeks." She nodded toward a lanky guy in his mid-twenties, messy sandy hair falling into his blue eyes, wearing a faded band tee under flannel. He was fiddling with the machine, tools scattered around him.

"Jasper Hale," he said, flashing a half-grin as he straightened up. "Don't bother with that thing. I keep trying to fix it, but it's deader than Ragina's conscience." He winked, his freckled face lighting up with mischief. "Welcome aboard, Emily. First-day survival tip: hide the stapler when the boss is on a rampage."

I laughed, feeling some of the tension ease. "Thanks. Sounds like I need all the tips I can get."

We chatted briefly as Felicity showed me the filing system. Jasper bounced ideas about streamlining project tracking, his energy infectious. For a moment, it felt like I might fit in here. The team seemed solid, Felicity's stoic strength complemented Jasper's jokes perfectly. Maybe this job would be the dream team I'd always wanted.

Then chaos erupted. The front door slammed open, and a sturdy woman in khakis and steel-toed boots stormed in, her short-cropped auburn hair streaked with gray, sharp hazel eyes blazing behind wire-rimmed glasses. She clutched a thick folder and marched straight to the center of the office.

"Where's Ragina Thomas?" she demanded, her voice a working-class twang thick with frustration. "I've had it up to here with these shell games. That invoice is sixty days past due, and my crew hasn't seen a dime!"

Felicity sighed, rubbing her temples. "Lila Hargrove. She's in a meeting. Calm down, she'll—"

"Calm down? My equipment loans are piling up, and RT's checks keep bouncing like bad rubber!" Lila slapped the folder on my desk. "Tell your boss to pay up, or I'm walking every site we have with them."

I glanced at the invoice; professional, detailed, for excavation work on a recent mall project. Sixty days overdue, all right. Before I could respond, the door to the corner office flew open.

Ragina Thomas emerged like a storm cloud in human form. Tall at 5'10", bottle-blonde hair teased high, piercing hazel eyes darting suspiciously under heavy makeup. She wore a designer power suit that must have cost two thousand dollars, straining at the seams, gold jewelry jangling with every step. Her manicured nails tapped aggressively against her thigh.

"What the hell is this?" Ragina shrieked, pointing a talon at Lila. "Extorting me in my own office? You think you can bully a woman running a business? This is MY company!"

Lila didn't flinch. "Extorting? Lady, you owe me thirty grand for dirt work that passed inspection. Pay up, or I'm filing liens on every one of your jobs."

Ragina's face twisted into a snarl. "Emily!" she barked, turning those wild eyes on me. I froze—three hours in, and she already knew my name. "You, new girl. Tell this sub the check is in the mail. We're mailing it today!"

Heart pounding, I opened the company banking app on my computer, as Felicity had shown me earlier. The balance stared back: twelve dollars and change. No pending checks, no outgoing wires. My stomach dropped. This was insane.

"Uh, Ragina, the account—" I started, but she cut me off with a wave.

"Just say it! The check is in the mail. Lie if you have to, that's what office managers do!" She leaned in close, her perfume overwhelming, voice dropping to a venomous hiss. "Do your job, or you're out on your ass."

I swallowed hard and relayed the message to Lila, who snorted in disgust. "In the mail, my ass. I've heard that bullshit for months." She stormed out, muttering about lawyers and small claims court.

Ragina straightened, smoothing her suit like nothing had happened. "See? Handled." She retreated to her office, slamming the door. The office fell silent, everyone avoiding eye contact.

Jasper leaned over. "Welcome to the shitshow. That woman's unhinged."

The rest of the afternoon dragged. I filed papers, organized client folders, trying to shake the unease gnawing at me. But as I sorted invoices, something caught my eye. Many had white-out corrections; dates changed, amounts inflated, vendor names scribbled over. Sloppy tampering, like someone had gotten desperate with correction fluid instead of digital edits. My hands shook slightly. This wasn't normal. I'd made a terrible mistake taking this job.

By 5 PM, my head throbbed from the tension. Felicity caught my eye. "Drinks? Local coffee shop down the street doubles as a bar after hours. You look like you need it."

I nodded gratefully. We slipped out, the coffee shop a cozy spot with worn booths and the rich aroma of fresh brews masking the underlying bitterness of cheap beer. We grabbed a corner table, ordered coffees laced with whiskey; Felicity's idea.

"First-day survival," she said, clinking mugs. Her direct, no-BS tone cut through the exhaustion. "I've got two kids counting on that paycheck, but fuck if this place isn't a nightmare."

I vented about the bank balance, the white-out, and Ragina's rage. Felicity listened, her maternal edge softening as we bonded over the chaos. "Ragina's not just mean," she warned, eyes serious. "She's dangerous. Paranoid as hell, thinks everyone's out to get her."

"What about the money? The account's empty. How does she keep the lights on?"

Felicity leaned in, voice low. "It's not just missing. It's being stolen—by the woman at the top. Forged statements, fake transfers. I've seen the trails. She's living like a queen while we scrape by. Watch your back, Emily. Once she trusts you, she'll drag you into the deep end."

Her words hit like ice water. This is white-collar crime, I thought. Fraud, right under my nose on day one. Felicity shared stories of bounced vendor checks, Ragina's manic rages where she'd hurl staplers and scream profanities. "She's got this delusion she's untouchable. But it's crumbling. Clients are bailing, subs like Lila are done."

We talked for hours, the whiskey loosening tongues. Felicity opened up about her divorce, the ex who drained their savings with addiction, how RT was her lifeline despite the red flags. "You're good people, Emily. But this place... it chews you up." Her dry wit emerged. "If Ragina were a site, it'd be condemned."

I laughed, but inside, dread built. Morally gray territory already—lying to Lila on orders, seeing the evidence of tampering. Trauma from my layoff made me cling to this job, but anxiety whispered to run.

Finally, we parted. Driving home, nausea hit hard. My apartment felt too quiet, the weight of the day pressing down. I collapsed on the couch, stomach churning. What the hell had I walked into? Ragina's shrill voice echoed, the empty bank balance burned in my mind. This wasn't a job; it was a powder keg. Sleep came fitfully, haunted by white-out ghosts and screaming suits.

The next morning, I stared at my closet, wondering if I could fake sick. But bills loomed, and quitting on day one screamed desperate. No, I'd play it smart, observe. Felicity's warning rang true—Ragina was dangerous, and the money trail led straight to her delusion. My high hopes were shattered, replaced by gritty resolve. Survive, document, maybe even expose. But for now, back to the circus.

That first day set the tone: camaraderie with Felicity and Jasper as lifelines, Ragina as the ticking bomb. The office image was a facade—professional on the surface, rotten beneath. Lila's storming exit foreshadowed more confrontations. And those altered invoices? Clues to a deeper fraud. My introspective drive kicked in, mentally cataloging details. This was no ordinary job; it was the start of a mystery I'd unravel, one tense day at a time.

As I drifted off, morally conflicted—loyalty to the team versus the crime staring me down—anxiety clawed deeper. Twelve dollars in the bank, a two-grand suit, lies about checks in the mail. White-collar hell, and I was in it now.

Bentleys and Bad Checks

Every day, we pull into the same parking lot with that gloomy gray building staring back at us. Every day, Felicity, Jasper, and I wonder how bad things will get. The only thing that keeps us showing up is our little team, the way we lean on each other through the chaos. Our group chat buzzes constantly with memes from Jasper and Felicity's dry warnings. But the management? It's a nightmare. Ragina Thomas runs RT Construction like her personal kingdom, and once you see behind the curtain, her name alone makes your skin crawl.

After my first-day disaster with Lila Hargrove and those white-out invoices, I dragged myself back the next morning, stomach still churning from Felicity's warnings over drinks. I promised myself I'd keep my head down, observe, survive. But day two hit like a freight train. I was at my desk, sorting through a stack of "Final Notice" utility bills that had piled up overnight. The electric was overdue by sixty days, the water was threatening shutoff. My anxiety spiked just looking at them. How was this company even functioning? Then I glanced out the window to the parking lot, and there she was.

Ragina pulled in driving a brand-new leased Bentley, the kind that screamed money no one in construction admin could afford. It was glossy black, shining under the morning sun, with those fancy rims spinning like they owned the asphalt. She stepped out in another power suit, this one red and straining, gold jewelry flashing as she slammed the door. The contrast hit me hard. That car cost more per month than my rent, while those bills mocked me from my desk. Where the hell is the cash coming from? I thought, my hands clenching the papers. Trauma from my layoff made every red flag feel like a personal attack, my mind racing with worst-case scenarios.

She strutted into the office like she owned the world—which she thought she did—her heels clicking sharply. "Staff meeting! Now!" she barked, voice shrill enough to shatter glass. We scrambled into the conference room, Felicity shooting me a knowing look, Jasper stifling a grin. Ragina stood at the head of the table, arms crossed, hazel eyes darting like she expected sabotage.

"Listen up, you incompetent fucks," she started, pacing with manic energy. "I just came back from the most high-stakes networking event in Vegas. Rubbed shoulders with the big boys—casino moguls, real estate tycoons. Deals are coming, people!" She bragged for ten minutes, name-dropping celebrities she'd clearly never met, waving her phone with selfies in front of slot machines she called "investment meetings." I realized instantly it was no networking trip. It was a gambling bender, funded straight from company coffers. My morally gray radar pinged hard. We were enabling this delusion, cashing checks from her fraud while pretending it was normal.

Her tone shifted, paranoia creeping in. "But somehow, money's leaking out of this place like a sieve. Clients dropping, vendors whining—it's all your fault! The office staff is bleeding me dry!" She slammed her fist on the table, eyes wild. Felicity tensed beside me, her stoic facade cracking just a bit. Jasper rolled his eyes subtly. Ragina jabbed a finger at us. "You're working overtime, unpaid, until we find every missing dime. Emily, you're organizing all the digital files. Clean that shit up. Everyone else, bill everything that moves. Do you know who I am? This is MY company!"

The meeting ended with her storming back to her private office, leaving us shell-shocked. "Unpaid overtime," Felicity muttered as we filed out. "That's some bullshit." Jasper leaned in. "Yeah, but did you see that Bentley? Networking my ass. She's got problems." I nodded, anxiety twisting my gut. Profanity flew in our group chat later: Jasper's "Boss lady living her best lie 😄" and Felicity's "Fuck this, kids need dinner, not her delusions."

I dove into the digital files as ordered, pulling up the shared drive on my computer. Folders upon folders of project docs, invoices, bank exports. Boring stuff until I hit one labeled "Marketing." Odd, since we had no marketing budget. I clicked in, and my heart stopped. It was stuffed with forged bank statements. Dozens of them, PDFs with RT Construction logos slapped on top. The numbers were inflated—balances showing six figures when I knew from yesterday the real account was scraping zero. But they were sloppy. The font was slightly off, a cheap Arial knockoff instead of the bank's standard. Headers were pixelated, like they'd been mocked up in a basic photo editor, not professional software. Watermarks were missing, dates mismatched. Anyone with half an eye could see they were fakes.

She's forging statements to hide the bleeding, I thought, pulse racing. This was white-collar crime staring me in the face, gritty and real. My hands shook as I screenshotted a few, saving them to a hidden thumb drive in my bag. Trauma from past jobs made me hesitate—was I digging my own grave? But the morally gray line we'd toed yesterday pushed me forward. Someone had to stop this.

That's when Jasper sidled up, his lanky frame leaning casually over my cubicle wall. He winked, that boyish grin masking his sharp eyes. "Find the motherlode?" he whispered, glancing around. Before I could answer, he pulled out his phone, showing a screenshot of a company credit card statement. Charges at a luxury boutique downtown: $4,200 on designer bags, $1,800 on shoes, all dated last week. While our office printer was out of ink, Ragina was dropping thousands on herself. "She's bleeding us for her high-roller bullshit," Jasper said, voice low and laced with profanity. "Gambling trips, Bentleys—fuckin' delusional."

We exchanged a look, a secret alliance forming in that moment. Jasper was no dumb jokester; he was whip-smart, spotting the same rot. "We gotta document this," I whispered back. "Quietly." He nodded, eyes twinkling with mischief but dead serious. "Group chat later. Felicity's gonna flip." It felt like the start of something, our little team against the empire. Dark comedy in the tension—laughing at the absurdity to keep the anxiety at bay.

Our plotting was cut short. Kendrick Blaise, the operations manager, loomed suddenly behind me. Stocky build, buzzed hair, hazel eyes narrowed like a predator. His company polo stretched over muscles, cargo pants stuffed with tools. He'd been Ragina's enforcer since day one, the guy who strong-armed subs like Lila. Now he leaned over my desk, way too close, his breath hot and laced with energy drink. The air thickened, his presence a physical threat. My fists clenched unconsciously, that coiled energy radiating menace.

"What the fuck are you poking at, new girl?" he growled, voice gruff and barked like an order. Street slang mixed with construction lingo. "Ragina said organize, not snoop. Mind your own goddamn business and fix the numbers like she asked." He jabbed a finger at my screen, close enough that I smelled his cheap cologne. My anxiety spiked, trauma flashing—visions of retaliation, job loss, worse. Kendrick wasn't just watching; he was deterring, Ragina's muscle keeping us in line.

I swallowed hard, forcing calm. "Just organizing, like she said." My voice stayed steady, but inside I was screaming. He lingered, staring me down, then snorted. "Fuckin' office pussies. Bill it all, or get your asses kicked off-site." He straightened, laughing mockingly as he walked away, but his eyes promised trouble. Jasper had vanished, playing dumb. Smart kid.

The rest of the day blurred into unpaid overtime hell. I shuffled files, eyes darting for more evidence, Kendrick's glare burning holes from across the room. Felicity texted: "Heard the growl. Stay frosty. Kids need me sane." Jasper sent a meme of a snarling dog captioned "Ops manager vibes." Dark humor kept us going, but the tension was gritty, real. Ragina's door stayed shut, probably admiring her Vegas selfies.

By evening, the parking lot emptied, the Bentley long gone. I sat alone, staring at the "Marketing" folder. Forged statements confirmed it: gambling debts funneled through shell games, personal splurges masked as business. The low-quality fakes screamed desperation. Kendrick's threat hung heavy, but Jasper's wink fueled me. Our alliance was sealed—we'd unravel this quietly, morally gray be damned.

Driving home, anxiety clawed deep. Profanity echoed in my head: Fuck this place. But quitting meant abandoning Felicity's kids' stability, Jasper's fresh start. No, we'd fight smart. The Bentley and bad checks were just the tip. White-collar crime, unraveling before me. My introspective drive cataloged every detail: sloppy fonts, boutique charges, threats. Ragina's empire was hollow, and we were the ones who'd expose it.

That night, group chat exploded.

Jasper: "Bentley bingo! Screenshot game strong. 😄👊"

Felicity: "Unpaid OT for her slots? Fuck no. I've got bills too."

I added my finds, heart pounding. Bonds tightened in digital shadows. Kendrick's watch, Ragina's rages—they amped the mystery, kept us guessing. But an alliance had formed, evidence mounting. Survival turned to subtle rebellion.

Days blurred into this rhythm: arrivals tense, meetings manic, digs discreet. Ragina bragged more, blamed harder. "You shits leaking my empire!" she'd shriek. We'd nod, screenshot, ally. Jasper's pranks lightened it—a fake "Out of Ink Fund" jar on her desk. Felicity's wit cut deep: "Her networking? More like net-losing." My anxiety? Chronic now, but channeled. Trauma fueled resolve, not flight.

One overtime night, Kendrick cornered Jasper in the break room. "Heard you cracking wise. Fix numbers or fuck off." Jasper played it cool. "Just billing EVERYTHING, boss. Therapy too? 😊" Kendrick shoved past, but we logged it. Physical deterrent confirmed—Ragina's paranoia had teeth.

Felicity pulled me aside later. "Careful with him. He's her dog on a short leash." Her maternal edge shone, voice direct. "But those forgeries? Gold for whoever's watching." A hint of her secrets, but I didn't push. Our alliance grew, three strong.

By week's end, I'd mapped the "Marketing" fakes: transfers to offshore accounts, boutique runs matching her Vegas timeline. Gambling confirmed—high-stakes slots draining RT dry. Printer ink? Forgotten. Our laughter turned gritty, profanity-laced vents becoming all too real.

Ragina called another meeting, Bentley parked proud. "More networking soon! Fix the leaks!" We smiled inside, knowing the truth. My alliance with Jasper solidified, Kendrick's threats a grim reminder. The circus rolled on, but now we had spotlights on the clowns.

Looking back, that Bentley day cracked it open. From naive newbie to insider detective, my arc began. Tension built organically, mystery deepening. Ragina's downfall loomed, one forged font at a time.

Amanda Ray

The Hidden Ledger

Every day started the same at RT Construction, with that gloomy gray building looming over the parking lot like a bad omen. Felicity, Jasper, and I would pull in together most mornings, sharing quick glances that said everything without words. The friendship we had built kept us going, turning the daily grind into something bearable through jokes in the group chat and quiet support. But after the Bentley fiasco and Kendrick's threats hanging over us like storm clouds, the tension felt thicker than ever. Ragina's forged statements and her delusional spending had us all on edge, wondering how deep the rot went. I spent every spare moment organizing those digital files, my eyes peeled for more clues while pretending to just follow orders.

That Wednesday, things took a sharp turn. I was at my desk mid-morning, sifting through another stack of vendor complaints, when Felicity appeared at the edge of my cubicle. Her sturdy frame filled the space, dark curls pulled tight in that no-nonsense bun, her deep brown eyes darting around to make sure no one was listening. She had that look, the one that said she was carrying a weight too heavy to ignore anymore. "Emily," she whispered, her voice low and clipped, Midwestern directness cutting through the office hum. "Supply closet. Now."

My heart skipped. Felicity wasn't one for dramatics; if she said now, it mattered. I nodded, grabbing a random ream of paper as cover, and followed her down the narrow hall. The supply closet was a cramped space stuffed with boxes of toner, stacks of printer paper, and dusty binders from years past. She slipped inside first, holding the door just wide enough for me to squeeze through, then pulled it shut behind us. The click of the lock echoed in the dim light, the air thick with the smell of ink and old cardboard. Her face was pale, those faint stretch marks on her arms visible as she rolled up her sleeves, like she was bracing for a fight.

"I've been keeping something," she said, her voice barely above a breath, eyes locked on mine with a mix of fear and resolve. "A secret record of every real transaction going back two years. I call it the Lifeboat Ledger. Started it when the first checks bounced, just to protect my kids if shit hit the fan." She paused, glancing at the door as if Ragina might burst through. "I'm terrified, Emily. If she finds out, she'll sue me into the ground or worse. Kendrick would make sure of it. But I can't watch the subcontractors like Lila go broke anymore. They're good people, working their asses off for nothing."

I felt a chill run down my spine. Felicity, the stoic powerhouse who juggled admin work and single-mom life without breaking a sweat, was cracking open her vault. "Show me," I whispered back, my anxiety spiking but curiosity winning out. This was the break we needed, the gritty proof behind all the suspicion.

She shook her head. "Not here. Too risky. Come to my place after work. We'll go through it all. Promise me you'll keep this between us." Her maternal edge came through, fierce and protective, like I was one of her own. I nodded, and we slipped out separately, her first to avoid suspicion. The rest of the day dragged, Kendrick's glares from across the room making my skin crawl, Jasper shooting me questioning looks in the group chat. I kept my head down, but my mind raced with possibilities. What if this ledger exposed everything? What if it pulled us deeper into the mess?

After work, I followed Felicity's sensible SUV to her modest house on the edge of town, a neat two-story with kids' bikes on the lawn and a minivan in the drive. Her place felt like a real home, warm lights spilling from the windows, the smell of spaghetti sauce greeting us at the door. Her two kids, energetic little ones with her curls and bright eyes, tumbled around until she shooed them to bed with promises of dessert later. "Thanks for watching them, Mom," one said, hugging her tight. That moment hit me—Felicity's stakes were sky-high, every risk she took tied to those smiles.

We settled in her cramped home office, a converted spare bedroom with a desk piled high with bills and toys. She pulled out a locked metal box from under the desk, her hands steady but eyes shadowed with anxiety. "This is it," she said, flipping it open to reveal a thick binder and a USB drive. Pages upon pages of meticulously copied invoices, bank statements, emails—everything timestamped and cross-referenced. "Every real dollar in and out, next to what Ragina reports. The gaps are her playground."

I flipped through, my stomach dropping as the scale hit me. Ragina wasn't just fudging numbers; she was orchestrating a full-blown fraud machine. "Look at this," Felicity pointed, her finger jabbing at a section labeled

Loans. "She's been taking out short-term, high-interest loans in our names. Without us knowing. Shell companies, fake approvals—it's identity theft on steroids."

My hands trembled as I grabbed her laptop, pulling up a secure database Felicity had mirrored from company records. "Search my name," I said, voice tight. The screen loaded, and there it was: an application for a fifty-thousand-dollar business loan, dated last month. My name, my social security number, even my address. But the signature at the bottom? A crude imitation of mine, wobbly lines that screamed forgery. "Holy shit," I breathed, leaning back as the realization hit like a physical blow. I was already an unwilling participant, my credit tangled in her web. If this blew up, I'd be on the hook too—ruined reputation, debt collectors at my door. Trauma from my layoff paled compared to this nightmare.

Felicity's face hardened, her dry wit surfacing through the fear. "Fuck if I'm going down with her sinking ship. I've got two kids counting on that paycheck. This ledger? It's our lifeboat." We dove in, cross-referencing forged docs with real expenses late into the night. Coffee went cold as numbers piled up. Ragina had stolen over four hundred thousand dollars in the last six months alone—loans funneled to her gambling sprees, Bentleys, Vegas "networking." Subcontractors stiffed, vendors suing, all while she played queen in her strained power suits.

"She's not just delusional," I said, rubbing my temples as anxiety clawed at me. "She's a goddamn thief.

Morally gray doesn't cover this—it's straight-up crime." Felicity nodded, her voice steady despite the tears welling. "I've bottled this for years, watching good people suffer. Anxiety eats at me every night, wondering if she'll come for my kids' future. But sharing it with you? Feels like fighting back."

We talked it through, voices hushed even in her quiet house. Felicity trusted me with her ultimate secret, her Lifeboat Ledger the key to unraveling it all. "You're resilient, Emily. Introspective but tough. We do this smart, or not at all." Her words fueled me, our bond deepening in that dimly lit room. Jasper would need to know soon, but tonight was ours—two women staring down an empire of lies.

By midnight, exhaustion hit, but resolve burned brighter. I couldn't just quit; that would leave me exposed, credit trashed, reputation in shreds. No, I had to bring the whole thing down, expose every forged signature and stolen cent. As Felicity locked the ledger away, I pulled the small encrypted drive from my keychain—a tiny thing I'd carried since my corporate days for sensitive files. "This is my log now," I said, plugging it in and starting entries: dates, docs, the loan in my name. Every detail, encrypted tight.

Driving home under streetlights, the weight settled. Ragina's paranoia, Kendrick's threats—it all made sense now. She wasn't just spending beyond her means; she was dragging us into felony territory. My mind replayed the forgery, that fake scrawl mocking me. I'm a victim too, I thought, anxiety twisting into anger. The office friendship that kept me there now demanded action.

White-collar crime, gritty and personal, had claimed its first casualty: my illusion of safety.

The next morning, the group chat lit up before I even parked.

Jasper: "Supply closet drama? Spill or meme incoming 😄."

Felicity: "Emily's place later. Big shit."

I added: "Ledger level 1000. Ragina forged MY signature. Loans in our names. We're fucked if we don't fight."

Profanity flew, dark comedy masking the trauma.

Jasper: "Identity theft party? Sign me up for revenge. 🤛"

Felicity: "Got those loan docs timestamped. Slow burn, team."

At the office, we played normal, but glances carried new weight. Kendrick loomed as usual, barking orders, but I met his glare now with steel. Ragina swept in late, jangling jewelry, oblivious. "Billing everything today!" she shrieked from her office. We nodded, but inside, the rebellion brewed. Felicity's trust changed everything; her secret ledger was our weapon.

Lunch was tense strategy in the break room. Jasper slid in, freckles dancing with his grin. "Spill the tea. Loans? For real?" Felicity laid it out low, her voice no-BS. "Four hundred K stolen, signatures faked. Emily's hit." His eyes widened, anxiety flashing before jokes kicked in. "Boss lady's playing Monopoly with our lives? Time to bankrupt her ass." We laughed, gritty relief cutting the fear.

Afternoon brought close calls. Kendrick hovered near Felicity's desk, grumbling about "pussy paper-pushers." She stared him down. "Got kids to feed, asshole. Back off." He snorted but retreated. I added to my drive: his intimidation, timestamped. Every moment documented, building our case.

By the end of the day, the ledger's shadow loomed large. Subcontractor Lila called, voice edged with desperation. "Another bounced check, Emily. Ragina's killing us." I soothed her, promising follow-up, my gut churning. Felicity's proof extended to her too—unpaid work fueling Ragina's delusions.

That night, alone with my drive, introspection hit hard. How did I miss this? Staying for friendship, cashing dirty checks—morally gray as hell. Anxiety kept me up, but purpose settled in. The Lifeboat Ledger wasn't just Felicity's; it was ours. Emily Harris, office manager turned reluctant detective, was all in. Ragina's empire would crumble, one forged line at a time.

We met again at Felicity's a few nights later, Jasper included now. Her kids asleep, we pored over more pages. "Look here," Jasper pointed, his lanky frame hunched. "Shell companies tied to her gambling markers." Felicity nodded. "Ledger caught it all." Cross-references revealed patterns: loans post-Vegas, fakes matching Bentleys. Over four hundred K, yes, but hints of more.

Emily's loan haunted me most. Fifty grand at predatory rates—if unpaid, my credit would tank. "She's stolen our futures," I said, voice raw. Felicity squeezed my shoulder, maternal strength flowing. "Not anymore. We're the lifeboat now." Jasper quipped, "Time to sink her ship. Feds incoming?" We shushed him, but the idea lingered.

Days blended, the office a minefield. Ragina ranted about "leaks," unaware her secrets had spilled. Kendrick's watch intensified, but we documented relentlessly. My keychain drive grew fat with files—screenshots, notes, the ledger scans Felicity shared securely.

One evening, as tension peaked, Felicity confessed more. "Bottled anxiety for years, trauma from my ex's addictions mirroring this shit. But trusting you? Best decision." Her vulnerability bonded us deeper, turning coworkers into family. Jasper admitted his panic too. "Jokes hide it, but this scares me shitless. Fresh grad, no backup."

I led now, introspective grit shining. "We expose it all. Credit be damned if we let her win."

Plans formed: anonymous tips, evidence drops. The mystery deepened, twists of identity theft fueling the fire. White-collar crime, personal and profane, demanded justice.

By week's end, my log was a robust, encrypted fortress against the storm.

Ragina's downfall brewed, our alliance unbreakable. The gloomy building held secrets no more; we'd lit the fuse.

Amanda Ray

A Very Expensive Lie

Every day at RT Construction felt like walking a tightrope over a pit of lies, but after Felicity's Lifeboat Ledger revelation, the ground beneath us shifted even more. Jasper, Felicity, and I exchanged loaded looks in the parking lot, our group chat buzzing with coded warnings and dark memes to keep the anxiety at bay. The forged loan in my name haunted my dreams, a constant reminder that Ragina's web had us all tangled. We kept up appearances, fielding furious calls from vendors like Lila Hargrove, who now texted me daily about bounced checks that threatened her crew's paychecks. Kendrick lurked like a storm cloud, his stocky frame casting shadows over our desks as he barked orders about fudged site reports. But beneath the routine, our secret alliance burned brighter, my encrypted drive growing fatter with every screenshot and note.

That Monday morning, the office hummed with the usual chaos—phones ringing off the hook, emails piling up with subcontractor complaints. I was knee-deep in collections when Ragina burst from her office like a hurricane in a power suit. Her bottle-blonde hair defied gravity, hazel eyes wild with that manic gleam we all dreaded. Gold jewelry jangled as she clapped her hands sharply, demanding attention. "Everyone! Meeting in the conference room! Now!" Her voice was shrill, laced with that delusional confidence that made my stomach twist. Jasper shot me a wide-eyed glance from his desk, his messy sandy hair falling into mischievous blue eyes, while Felicity rolled hers, her sturdy build already tensing under her sensible blouse.

We filed into the cramped conference room, the air thick with cheap coffee and unspoken dread. Ragina stood at the head of the table, talons tapping impatiently on a glossy brochure she'd slapped down. "It's our anniversary! Fifteen years of RT Construction dominating this city!" she announced, her chest puffing out against the straining seams of her suit. "And I'm throwing the biggest gala this town has ever seen—at the Luxe Grand Hotel ballroom. The most expensive spot in the city! Black-tie, champagne fountains, the works!" Her smile was predatory, eyes darting as if daring us to challenge her.

Jasper leaned over, whispering under his breath, "Champagne fountains? In our budget? This is gonna be lit... or bankrupt us." I stifled a gritty laugh, but anxiety clawed at my chest. Vendors were screaming for payments, our real accounts scraped bare, and now this? Felicity crossed her arms, her deep brown eyes narrowing. "Sounds amazing, Ragina," she said, her voice direct and no-BS, "but we're swamped with angry calls. Who's handling planning?"

Ragina waved it off like swatting a fly. "You four! My dream team! Emily, you're on point—book it today. Deposit's ten grand. Use the company card." She thrust the brochure at me, her manicured nails gleaming. My heart sank. I knew our books inside out; that card was a joke, tied to accounts Felicity's ledger proved were illusions. "Ragina," I said carefully, my conversational grit masking the tremor, "we can't afford the deposit. The vendors are piling up lawsuits, banks are freezing everything. This gala... it's not realistic right now."

The room went dead silent. Ragina's face twisted, hazel eyes bulging as paranoia flashed. "What did you say?" she hissed, voice rising to a shriek. "You think I can't afford it? I have millions in offshore accounts! Temporarily frozen by those sexist bankers who hate a strong woman like me!" Her fists clenched, jewelry clinking furiously. Before I could respond, she snatched a heavy glass paperweight from the table—a gaudy crystal thing shaped like a skyscraper—and hurled it at the wall. It shattered with a deafening crash, shards raining down like her crumbling facade. "You little shits are trying to sabotage me! This is MY company! Fix it or you're all fired!" Spit flew, her body shaking in a volcanic meltdown. Kendrick smirked from the corner, his goatee twitching, but even he shifted uncomfortably.

We scattered as she stormed out, slamming the door. In the hallway, Jasper's half-grin faltered. "Offshore millions? She's lost it. That's some next-level delusion." Felicity nodded, her maternal edge sharpening. "I've seen the ledger—that's bullshit. But we play along, document everything." My hands shook as I grabbed the phone, dialing the Luxe Grand under Ragina's glare from her office window. "Yes, the ballroom for fifty guests. Deposit ten thousand," I told the events coordinator, reading off the company card number. My pulse thundered; it would decline, exposing her lie right there. But to my horror— and twisted surprise—the line went silent, then: "Approved. Thank you, Ms. Harris."

I hung up, staring at the screen as the transaction confirmation pinged. How? Digging into our fractured accounting system, cross-referencing Felicity's Lifeboat data, I found it: a new "emergency" loan, fifty thousand at thirty percent interest, routed through a shady lender with ties to one of Ragina's shell companies. Predatory as hell, the kind that ruined lives. My anxiety spiked—this wasn't just spending; it was digging a deeper grave, with us shoveling. "It went through," I whispered to the team huddle by the copier. "Another goddamn loan. Thirty percent. She's funding fairy tales with our blood."

Ragina, oblivious or uncaring, spent the rest of the day preening. She vanished mid-morning for a "makeover," returning with fresh highlights and layers of makeup that couldn't hide the strain. Then her credit card swiped again—this time for a five-thousand-dollar gown from some designer boutique, delivered in a garment bag that screamed excess. "For the gala!" she crowed, parading it through the office. "You peasants wouldn't understand true class." Her boasts grated, each one a knife twist amid our vendor hell. Lila called again while Ragina admired herself in a mirror. "Emily, my crew's walking off-site. No pay, no dirt moved." I soothed her, promising checks tomorrow, but guilt gnawed—morally gray didn't cover enabling this.

Meanwhile, Jasper poked around Kendrick's office during a "smoke break" diversion Felicity staged. He returned pale, lanky frame slouched, holding a crumpled box of shredder confetti. "Guys... check this." We huddled in the supply closet again, sorting bits under fluorescent light. Fragments of federal tax forms—1099s, W-2s, schedules riddled with alterations. "She's not just failing," Jasper said, voice cracking, "she's evading taxes on a massive scale. Hiding income through shells, underreporting everything. That's federal-prison shit."

The realization hit like a freight train. Ragina wasn't a bad businesswoman; she was a criminal mastermind unraveling. White-collar crime at its grittiest—tax evasion layered on fraud, loans, forgeries. My introspective mind reeled: we'd been complicit, cashing checks from this poison. Trauma from my layoff felt quaint compared to this anxiety vortex. Felicity's face hardened. "Ledger matches. She's cooked." But Jasper... his boyish grin vanished, freckles stark against flushed skin. He slid down the wall, breath hitching. "This is too much. Feds, prison, my career... I can't..." A panic attack gripped him, chest heaving, eyes wild.

Felicity dropped to her knees, maternal instinct kicking in. "Breathe, kid. In through your nose, out through your mouth. We've got you." I knelt too, gripping his shoulder. "Jasper, you're not alone. Jokes aside, you're our glue. This stress? It's breaking us all, but we fight smarter." His rapid-fire quips silenced by gasps, he clutched my arm. "Feels like home all over again—chaos, no escape. What if we lose everything?" Dark comedy failed him; raw trauma spilled. Profanity-laced sobs: "Fuck this job, fuck her empire." We held him through it, the closet a confessional for our collective mental health crumble. Felicity wiped tears, admitting, "Mortgage statements last night... I cried over bills, kids' faces in my head. This anxiety's a bitch."

Back at our desks, Ragina preened over her gown bag, oblivious. "Gala will save us! Investors incoming!" Delusional rants echoed. Kendrick eyed us suspiciously, but we documented—shredder pics on my drive, loan details logged. Jasper rallied with a weak meme in chat: "Tax evasion party? I'm out 😄." But his hands still shook. I managed Ragina's mania all afternoon, dodging her demands for invites to "celebrities" she'd name-dropped. One meltdown had her screaming at a mirror: "They hate me because I'm a woman!" Glass-shattering rage, then saccharine charm: "Emily, book the caviar. Offshore funds thaw soon."

By closing, exhaustion settled like fog. Felicity hugged Jasper goodbye, her stoic powerhouse cracking. "Kids tonight—normalcy anchor." He nodded, masking anxiety with a grin. Driving home, I replayed it all: the gala lie, predatory loan miracle, tax shreds, Jasper's breakdown. Ragina's empire, built on expensive deceptions, teetered. Our team, bonded in trauma, bore the weight. Morally gray choices haunted me—stay silent or risk it all? My drive hummed with evidence, first-person resolve hardening. This gala would be her Waterloo, one glittering lie at a time.

The next day amplified the toll. Ragina strutted in, basking in her makeover glory, barking gala tweaks amid vendor voicemails. "Lila again?" she sneered when I mentioned it. "Tell her to fuck off—pay her after the party!" Her profanity flew, unfiltered narcissism. Jasper hovered near the break room, eyes distant. Felicity pulled mortgage statements from her bag, tears streaking as she calculated. "One more bounced influx, and eviction looms. Fuck her frozen accounts." Strong language vented our grit, profanity a release valve for bottled rage.

I confronted Ragina privately, managing her derangement. "The loan's at thirty percent—it's killing us." She laughed, shrill. "Details! I've got millions waiting!" Paranoia flickered. "You believe me, right? Not like those traitors." Chills ran down my spine; her hazel eyes pierced, makeup cracking at the edges. Meanwhile, Jasper sorted more shreds, piecing together the tax-evasion puzzle. "Deductions faked for gambling 'business trips.' Massive scale." Our discovery fueled purpose amid anxiety—mental health fraying, but justice calling.

The break room became a sanctuary. Jasper confessed deeper: "Panic hit like a truck. Trauma from Dad's mess—bills, fights. This mirrors it." Felicity shared, "My ex's addiction drained us; now this. Crying over statements? Rock bottom." I nodded, introspective. "My forged loan? Anxiety nightmare. But together? We're unbreakable." Dark comedy laced it. Jasper's "Gala of Doom: Dress code—handcuffs" drew weak laughs. Team support wove tighter, morally gray lines blurring toward heroism.

Ragina's day ended with gown fittings in her office, mirror-gazing boasts. "Five grand well spent! Offshore billions thaw soon." Lies piled up, but her volcanic core simmered. We clocked out, group chat alive.

Felicity: "Shreds timestamped."

Jasper: "Panic over, revenge mode 🔥."

Me: "Gala's her noose. Log it all."

The tension stayed gritty, serious, laced with profane resolve. White-collar unraveling had left us scarred, but alive—ready for the empire's fall.

Amanda Ray

The Traitor's Note

The morning after Ragina's gala delusions hit peak insanity, the office felt like a powder keg with a lit fuse. Jasper, Felicity, and I dragged ourselves in, our group chat still humming from last night's stress vents—Jasper's panic-attack memes mixed with Felicity's no-BS reminders to "breathe and document." The air was thick with unspoken dread, vendors like Lila Hargrove blowing up my phone about her crew's walkout threats. We settled at our desks, pretending normalcy while Kendrick's stocky shadow loomed, his buzzed head swiveling like a guard dog. Ragina was nowhere in sight yet, but her presence hung heavy, that five-thousand-dollar gown probably still draped in her office like a delusional trophy.

Then the phone rang. Not our usual vendor rage—the main line, shrill and insistent. I picked up, my voice steady from months of this bullshit. "RT Construction, Emily speaking." A distorted voice, low and gravelly, crackled through. "Yeah, connect me to the fraud department." My blood ran cold. Fraud department? Before I could process, Ragina exploded from her office, bottle-blonde hair wilder than usual, hazel eyes blazing. She snatched the receiver from my hand. "Who the fuck is this?" she screamed, her voice piercing the room. The line went dead. She slammed the phone down, face twisting in rage. "A spy! There's a goddamn traitor in this building!"

Paranoia ignited like dry tinder. Ragina paced the main office area, her designer heels clicking furiously on the linoleum, gold jewelry jangling with every agitated step. She loomed over Jasper's desk first, her talons gripping the back of his chair as she peered at his screen.

"What the hell are you typing, boy? Deleting shit?" Jasper's lanky frame stiffened, his sandy hair flopping as he minimized a spreadsheet with feigned casualness.

"Just vendor logs, Ragina. Nothing shady." She snorted, moving to Felicity, who sat ramrod straight, her tight dark curls in that no-nonsense bun, deep brown eyes unflinching. "Collections? Or calling the cops?" Felicity's voice was direct, Midwestern and clipped. "Fuck no, just chasing payments for your crew."

I felt her breath hot on my neck next, scanning my monitor where the Lifeboat Ledger hid in encrypted tabs. My heart hammered, anxiety spiking like it had during Jasper's break-room meltdown yesterday. She can't know. Not yet. "Emily, my dream team leader—plotting my downfall?" Her tone dripped saccharine venom. I forced a smile, conversational grit masking the trauma churning inside. "Just gala invites, Ragina. Hotel confirmed, deposit cleared." She lingered too long, then spun away, muttering about "backstabbers" and "sexist sabotage."

That's when she found it. In the common area by the coffee machine—a crumpled scrap of paper, handwritten in block letters: "I know what you're doing." Ragina snatched it up, her face draining of color before flushing crimson. "This! This is for me! One of you fuckers wrote this!" The room froze. Jasper shot me a wide-eyed glance, freckles stark against pale skin; Felicity's sturdy build tensed, maternal worry flashing for her kids. Kendrick smirked from his corner, goatee twitching, but even his hazel eyes narrowed. Ragina crumpled the note in her fist. "No one leaves. No one!" She bolted to the front door, deadbolting it with a heavy thunk, then stormed to the back exit, locking that too. The office transformed into a cage, windows mocking us with outside freedom.

"We're finding the traitor now," Ragina snarled, her imposing 5'10" frame blocking the hall. "One by one, into my office. Interrogations start with you, Jasper!" Terror rippled through us. We shared a look—pure, shared horror. Jasper's half-grin vanished; Felicity mouthed stay strong; my stomach knotted with morally gray guilt. We'd been feeding the feds crumbs for months, but this? This was the noose tightening. Jasper slouched after her, shoulders hunched, while the rest of us sat in stunned silence, the locked doors amplifying every creak and whisper.

Minutes stretched like hours. Jasper emerged first, face ashen, muttering "She's lost it" under his breath. Felicity went next, her cross-trainers silent on the carpet. "Keep it together," she whispered to me en route, her gold wedding band glinting—a reminder of her own trauma from that addict ex. Kendrick's turn came with barked defiance; he slammed the door, voices muffled but heated. "Loyal, boss! Fuck these paper-pushers!" My anxiety built, palms slick, mind racing through contingencies. The drive. If she finds it... Trauma from the forged loan, the tax shreds—it all swirled in a gritty mental-health storm.

Finally, my turn. "Emily! Now!" Ragina's shrill command echoed. I rose on shaky legs, messenger bag heavy with my secret encrypted keychain drive. Her office door loomed like a portal to hell. Inside, darkness enveloped everything—blinds drawn, only a desk lamp casting eerie shadows. Ragina sat slumped in her leather chair, clutching a bottle of top-shelf bourbon, the label screaming excess amid our poverty. Her power suit strained, makeup smudged, hazel eyes glinting like a predator's in the gloom. The air reeked of booze and desperation, her voluminous hair deflating like her empire.

"Sit," she hissed, pointing to the chair opposite. I obeyed, heart pounding against my ribs. Profanity bubbled in my throat, but I swallowed it, introspective voice in my head screaming, Play dumb, survive. She slid a paper across the desk—a printed copy of my personal bank statement. My real one, not company bullshit. Transactions highlighted: coffee runs, rent, that anonymous tip-line deposit to the feds. "How the fuck did you get this?" I blurted, voice cracking with genuine shock. She'd hacked it illegally, no doubt—some shady PI or dark-web pull, white-collar crime layered on felony privacy breach.

Ragina's lips curled into a cold, terrifying smile, talons tapping the bourbon bottle. "I know everything, Emily. You've been talking to people outside the company. Cops? Feds? Vendors stirring shit?" Her voice rose, paranoia in overdrive. "That anonymous call? Your doing!" I shook my head, anxiety fueling a gritty denial. "Ragina, that's insane. I'm loyal—gala, vendors, all of it." But she laughed, shrill and unhinged, leaning forward. Her hand plunged into her desk drawer, emerging with my keychain drive—the small, innocuous USB disguised as a trinket on my desk for months, fat with Lifeboat Ledger scans, wire fakes, tax shreds.

She dangled it between two manicured fingers, gold rings flashing. "Did you think I wouldn't notice a new toy on your desk? Cute. Encrypted, too—real spy shit." My world tilted. Morally gray blurred to black; this was endgame. Trauma hit hard—flashes of Jasper's panic, Felicity's tears, my own forged-loan nightmare. She's deranged. Pure mental-health abyss. Profanity-laced thoughts raced: Fuck, fuck, fuck. The team outside, locked in terror; Lila's crew starving on bounced checks; Ragina's narcissistic empire crumbling, taking us down.

"Password," she demanded, rising slowly, drive in hand. Her face twisted into a mask of pure derangement—eyes bulging, makeup cracking like her facade, bourbon breath hot and foul. She moved toward the computer, hips swaying with menacing intent, heels scraping the floor. "Unlock it now, traitor, or I bury you all. This is my company!" The lamp light carved shadows on her imposing frame, turning her into a monster from our collective anxiety dreams. I gripped the chair arms, strong language bottled inside, waiting for the explosion. Her talon hovered over the keyboard, drive poised to plug in. The bourbon bottle clinked against the desk, forgotten in her rage. Outside, muffled voices—Jasper, Felicity, Kendrick—strained against the locked doors, oblivious to my unraveling.

But in that dark room, time slowed. Ragina's paranoia had built for months—losing clients to her ops clowns Jesse and William, fake wires, predatory loans at thirty percent, tax-evasion shreds Jasper pieced together. We'd endured her rages, her victim plays: "They hate me 'cause I'm a woman!" Now, this. My mind flashed to our friendship, the only light in this hell—bouncing ideas with Jasper like siblings, Felicity's stoic strength mirroring a big sister's, our group chat a lifeline amid the grit. Dark comedy had kept us sane: Jasper's "Gala of Doom" memes after her paperweight smash. But this confrontation stripped it bare, exposing the raw trauma we'd bottled.

She leaned closer, drive twirling. "Talk, Emily. Or watch your little team burn." Her cold smile returned, terrifying in the dimness. Anxiety clawed my chest, mental health fraying at the edges—morally gray choices haunting me: snitch and risk retaliation, or lie and dig deeper? The note in the common area replayed—"I know what you're doing"—maybe Lila, maybe a fed plant, but it lit her fuse. The locked doors echoed our prison, the staff's terror-stricken looks burned in memory. Ragina's hazel eyes bored into mine, deranged mask complete, demanding the password as she inched toward the computer.

I swallowed hard, gritty resolve flickering. The bourbon's amber glow mocked our empty accounts. Her talons clicked on the drive, poised. Tension peaked, every breath heavy with the weight of white-collar crimes unraveling. This was it—the traitor's note had cracked her wide open, and now my secret stared back from her fingers.

Amanda Ray

Under the Thumb

My heart hammered against my ribs like it was trying to break free from my chest. Ragina loomed over her desk in the dim light of her office, that encrypted keychain drive dangling from her talons like a death sentence. Her face was a twisted mask of derangement, hazel eyes wild with bourbon-fueled paranoia, the expensive bottle sweating on the desk beside her. "Password," she snarled again, inching closer to the computer, her designer heels scraping the floor like nails on a chalkboard. The air reeked of her perfume mixed with booze, thick and suffocating. Outside, I knew Jasper, Felicity, and even Kendrick were trapped behind those locked doors, oblivious to how close we were to total exposure.

I had seconds. My mind raced through every lie I'd ever told, every morally gray choice that got me here. The Lifeboat Ledger on that drive—our secret record of fake wires, forged loans, tax-evasion scraps—was our lifeline to the feds. If she cracked it, we were done. Thinking fast, I let my eyes well up, channeling every ounce of fake vulnerability I could muster. I thought of Felicity's single-mom strength, her kids counting on that paycheck, and twisted it into my performance. "Please, Ragina," I whispered, my voice cracking as I pulled a photo from my messenger bag—one of my niece and nephew from last Christmas, innocent smiles that could melt anyone. "That drive... it's not what you think. It's just photos of my kids. Family memories. I didn't want them on the work computer, in case something happens to it. Please don't look. They're all I have."

Tears spilled down my cheeks, hot and real now from the sheer anxiety clawing at my gut. I played the terrified aunt—close enough to single-mom desperation without lying outright—hunching my shoulders, hands trembling as I clutched the photo. Ragina paused, her imposing frame freezing mid-step. Her narcissistic ego lit up like a spotlight; she lived for dominance, for making people beg. A scoff escaped her painted lips, loud and dismissive. "Your kids? Pathetic. Look at you, weeping over some snot-nosed brats while my empire burns because of traitors like you." She tossed the drive back across the desk, where it skidded to a stop near my hand. Boredom flickered in her eyes—she craved bigger prey, not some "sad sack mommy drama." "Get out. All of you, back to work. But know this: I've installed keyloggers on every goddamn computer. One wrong keystroke, one email to your fed buddies, and you're all fucked."

I snatched the drive, stuffing it into my bag with shaking fingers, and bolted from the room. Relief hit like a wave, but it was laced with trauma—my pulse thundered, stomach churning with the what-ifs. Had she bought it fully? The locked doors clicked open as Ragina bellowed from her office, "Meeting over! No one breathes without my say-so!" Jasper shot me a wide-eyed thumbs-up from his desk, his lanky frame slouched in feigned casualness, freckles pale against his skin. Felicity's deep brown eyes met mine, a nod of stoic understanding passing between us. Even Kendrick grunted, his stocky build unclenching slightly, though his hazel eyes narrowed suspiciously. We scattered to our desks, the office air electric with unspoken victory and dread.

The next morning, the office felt like a prison straight out of some gritty white-collar nightmare. Gray walls closed in tighter, fluorescent lights buzzing like interrogators. Kendrick stalked the aisles now, his steel-toed boots thudding with purpose, buzzed head swiveling as he loomed over shoulders. No more group chat pings, no casual banter—his coiled energy screamed surveillance. "Eyes on screens, mouths shut," he barked at Jasper, who was pretending to crunch vendor numbers. Jasper's half-grin faltered, but he nodded, his blue eyes darting to me in silent panic. Felicity typed furiously, her sturdy mom jeans creaking as she shifted, but even her dry wit stayed bottled. Me? Anxiety gnawed at my insides, a constant mental-health hum—every keystroke felt watched, every glance a risk.

We needed to communicate, to get the evidence out before the keyloggers snagged us. Jasper caught my eye first, slipping a sticky note under a stack of invoices on my desk:

Fax? Back room?

Genius. I scribbled back:

Yes. Lifeboat pages. Flush after.

We passed them like contraband—me to Felicity during a fake coffee run, her maternal edge shining as she pocketed it without a word. Kendrick prowled closer once, his goatee twitching as he growled, "No chit-chat, ladies." We froze, hearts pounding, but he moved on, fists clenching unconsciously. In the office kitchen, amid the drip of the ancient coffee maker, Jasper and I huddled by the sink. "This is some spy-movie shit," he whispered, voice rapid-fire with a dark-comedy edge. "But for real, Em, if he catches us..." I nodded, trauma flashing—Ragina's deranged smile, the bourbon stench. "Flush everything. We're ghosts now."

That's when I remembered the old fax machine in the back storage room, a dusty relic Ragina swore was broken after she "upgraded" to digital everything. It sat under a pile of yellowed manuals, its paper tray warped but intact. Felicity's brother, a tech guy with shady connections, had set up a dedicated receive line weeks ago—just in case. Perfect. Heart racing like I was defusing a bomb, I snuck back there during lunch, Kendrick's footsteps echoing too close in the hall. The machine whirred to life with a groan, lights flickering like it resented the intrusion. I fed in the first pages of the Lifeboat Ledger—scans of fake wire transfers, shell-company loans at predatory rates, tax docs Jasper had pieced together from shreds. Each beep felt like a gunshot, the paper inching through slow as molasses. Come on, you ancient piece of crap, I thought, sweat beading on my forehead, anxiety spiking with every whir.

Twenty pages in, Kendrick's shadow darkened the doorway. "Harris! What the fuck are you doing back here?" His voice was a gruff, profane bark echoing off the boxes. I yanked the page mid-send, heart slamming. "Just... clearing junk. Ragina said declutter." He stepped closer, a tattoo peeking from his collar, muscles straining his polo. Suspicion burned in his eyes, but the machine's hum masked the fax tone. "Move it. Boss wants reports." He grabbed my arm—hard enough to bruise—and dragged me out. I flushed the sticky-note remnants in the bathroom, hands shaking, morally gray relief washing over me. It worked. Pages one through twenty were out, en route to freedom.

The rest of the day dragged in tense silence. Jasper slipped me another note during a vendor-call distraction:

More tonight? Risky.

I nodded subtly, but inside, the prison vibe crushed us. Felicity cornered me by the fridge later, her practical watch ticking relentlessly. "Kids need me home," she muttered, voice clipped with maternal fury. "This keylogger bullshit—fuck it. Fax more if you can." Her deep brown eyes held quiet strength, but I saw the bottled anxiety, the trauma of her ex's addiction mirroring this chaos. Jasper hovered nearby, energy drink in hand, whispering, "Pizza run later? Cover?" His optimistic prankster side cracked through, but his freckled face was drawn, ramen-diet fears unspoken yet.

After hours, with Kendrick finally clocking out, we reconvened in the back. The fax whirred again, devouring pages thirty to fifty—evidence of Ragina's gambling shells disguised as "networking," bounced vendor checks to folks like Lila Hargrove. Each transmission was agony; the machine jammed twice, paper crinkling loudly, forcing Jasper to stand guard. "Hear that? Footsteps," he hissed once, blue eyes wide. False alarm, but my pulse didn't recover. We flushed notes in batches, the toilet gulping our secrets. By the fiftieth page, sweat soaked my blouse, anxiety at a fever pitch. One slip, and we're accessories. Morally gray? This is survival.

Ragina swept through once, her voluminous blonde hair still defying gravity, power suit straining as she inspected. "Keyloggers catching anything?" she demanded of Kendrick, who shook his head. "Clean, boss. These pussies know better." She sneered at us, jangling gold clinking. "Good. One traitor, and I burn it all." Her paranoia fed the tension, her narcissistic victim play in full swing: "They hate me because I'm a woman entrepreneur!" We nodded meekly, but inside, dark comedy bubbled—Jasper's later text (burner phone, off-network): Queen of Delusions strikes again 😄 But fr, we're winning.

As the sun dipped, the final pages faxed through—the complete Lifeboat Ledger, our white-collar bomb ticking toward detonation. I powered down the machine, burying it again, chest heaving. We'd conned the monster, dodged the enforcer, leaked the truth. But the office prison lingered, Kendrick's surveillance a constant threat. My hands trembled with the post-adrenaline crash, trauma settling like lead—nights of anxiety dreams ahead, replaying her deranged demand. Yet, for the first time in months, hope flickered. The feds had it now. Ragina's thumb was slipping.

Back at my desk, Jasper high-fived discreetly, Felicity's stoic nod sealing our bond. The group chat—burner edition—lit up later:

Fax success. Lifeboat away. Hold tight.

Profanity-laced relief poured in, gritty humor masking the mental-health toll. We'd survived another day under the thumb, but the noose loosened just a fraction. Tomorrow? More risks, more sticky notes, more whirring defiance. This was our fight—friends against the deranged empire, one fax at a time.

The Ghost of Payroll

Friday morning hit like a gut punch, and we all dragged ourselves into the parking lot of that same gloomy gray building. Every week, payday was supposed to be the light at the end of the tunnel, but with Ragina Thomas running the show at RT Construction, it felt more like another trap waiting to spring. I parked next to Felicity's sensible minivan, her tight dark curls already pulled into that no-nonsense bun, and Jasper's beat-up truck with its faded band stickers. We exchanged tired nods, the weight of the past week's prison-like surveillance hanging over us like a storm cloud. The Lifeboat Ledger pages were out via that ancient fax machine, but payday loomed, and hope flickered thin against the anxiety gnawing at my insides.

Inside the office reception, the air was thick with expectation as we gathered around the front desk. Ragina swept in late, her bottle-blonde hair teased high, designer suit straining at the seams, gold jewelry jangling like warning bells. She carried a stack of what looked like certificates, her hazel eyes darting suspiciously as if we were all plotting her downfall. "Listen up, you ungrateful shits," she barked, slamming the pile down. "The bank fucked up again—some clerical error. Paychecks delayed seventy-two hours. But here's your loyalty certificates! Proof you're part of my empire. Cash 'em next week, or better yet, frame 'em!" Her voice rose to a shrill pitch, narcissistic delusion radiating off her as she thrust one into my hands. It was worthless paper, printed on the office laser printer, promising "future compensation" from RT Construction.

This was the third time in two months. The first delay, we chalked it up to a glitch. The second, Ragina blamed "sexist bankers." Now, it was just her crumbling schemes laid bare. Felicity's sturdy frame went rigid, her deep brown eyes filling with quiet devastation. She clutched the certificate, her practical watch ticking relentlessly on her wrist. "Ragina, my mortgage is due Monday," she said, her voice clipped, Midwestern directness laced with profanity waiting to erupt. "Kids' school fees too. This isn't funny." Ragina scoffed, waving her manicured talons. "Figure it out, single mom. I've got vacations to fund—real business expenses!" Felicity's face paled, the stoic powerhouse cracking as she turned away, bottling the anxiety that mirrored her ex-husband's addiction-fueled chaos.

Jasper leaned against the reception counter, his lanky 6'1" frame slouched, messy sandy hair falling into his twinkling blue eyes. He tried his half-grin, but it faltered. "Boss, I'm down to ramen packets. Literal ramen. My truck payment's gonna bounce." His rapid-fire quip hid the trauma of his chaotic upbringing, but his freckled face showed real strain. Ragina whirled on him. "Ramen builds character, boy! Do you know who I am? This is MY company!" She stormed off to her office, leaving the mood toxic, the air sucked dry of any camaraderie we'd scraped together.

The office turned into a graveyard. No one spoke; Kendrick's surveillance had us all jumping at shadows. Felicity retreated to her desk, furiously typing collections emails that would never collect. Jasper stared at his screen, memes unspoken. I paced the reception area, anxiety spiking—morally gray choices piling up, like staying for these friends while feeding the feds. Then Kendrick lumbered in from the sites, his stocky build filling the doorway, buzzed head gleaming under fluorescents. "Cheer up, pussies," he grunted, gruff voice barking like orders. He plunked down greasy boxes of cheap pizza on the reception table—Domino's knockoff, cold and congealing. "Boss's treat. Eat up." His hazel eyes narrowed, goatee twitching, as if this macho gesture would erase the payroll ghost haunting us. Nobody touched it. Felicity shot him a maternal glare. "Not hungry," she muttered. Jasper poked a slice. "Looks like the fake wires—greasy and full of lies." Kendrick's fists clenched, but he just laughed mockingly and stomped off.

The tension simmered until the lobby doors burst open. Lila Hargrove strode in, her short-cropped auburn hair streaked gray, sturdy 5'6" build clad in khakis and steel-toed boots, faded tattoos peeking from rolled sleeves. Flanking her was a sharp-suited lawyer, briefcase in hand, ready for war. Lila's hazel eyes burned behind wire-rimmed glasses—this subcontractor had endured too many bounced checks. "Ragina Thomas!" Lila called, working-class twang clipped and blunt. "Time to pay up. Lawsuit served for unpaid invoices. I've had it up to here with your shell games." The lawyer stepped forward, papers extended, providing a slice of outside reality crashing into our office chaos.

Chaos erupted. Kendrick exploded from the back, his coiled energy unleashing as he physically blocked the lawyer, stocky frame a human wall. "No fucking way," he growled, profane street slang mixing with construction lingo. "You ain't serving shit in here. Get out!" He planted steel-toed boots wide, tattooed forearm shoving the lawyer back. Lila didn't flinch. "Put the hammer down, muscle boy. We've got timelines, ledgers—your boss owes my crew six figures." The shouting match filled the lobby, voices bouncing off gray walls. Ragina shrieked from her office, "Kendrick, handle it!" Jasper and Felicity hovered, wide-eyed, the distraction a godsend.

This was my moment. Heart pounding, anxiety a fever in my veins, I slipped to the reception counter. I'd hidden a thumb drive in a pack of gum—more Lifeboat Ledger backups, wire-transfer proofs, forged-loan docs—tucked in my messenger bag. Amid the yells, I palmed it, sidled to Lila during a lull. "Here," I whispered, pressing the gum pack into her callused hand. "District Attorney's office. Quiet." Her sharp eyes met mine, pragmatic resilience flashing understanding. She nodded once, pocketing it without a word, her arc from tolerant vendor to whistleblower sealing in that glance. Risking everything for this pass—morally gray treason against Ragina, loyalty to my team—sent trauma-fueled adrenaline surging. The lawyer shouted, "Assault! We're calling the cops!" Kendrick bellowed back, fists raised, buying us seconds.

Ragina finally emerged, voluminous hair defying gravity, power suit askew. "Out! All of you! Kendrick, escort 'em!" He manhandled them toward the doors, the lawyer protesting, Lila shooting me a final look of grim alliance. The lobby cleared, pizza congealing untouched, certificates mocking us from the desk. Felicity exhaled shakily. "Fuck, Em. That was ballsy." Jasper high-fived discreetly. "Spy shit level 100. But my ramen life calls." Dark comedy laced our whispers, but the toxicity lingered, the ghost of payroll rattling chains.

The day dragged, the office a pressure cooker. Ragina locked herself away, paranoia fueling rants audible through the walls: "Traitors everywhere! Women like me get screwed!" We worked in silence, flushing sticky notes, anxiety humming. Felicity vented in a hushed group-chat ping—burner phones only: "Mortgage notice incoming. Kids asking why no groceries. This trauma's real." Jasper replied with a meme, but his texts screamed instability fears. I stared at my screen, introspective grit churning—how many more delays before we broke? Profanity bubbled internally: Fuck this deranged bitch and her empire of lies.

Quitting time came like mercy. I bolted to the parking lot, chestnut bob whipping in the wind, scuffed flats pounding pavement. My worn messenger bag bounced heavy with secrets. Driving home, the mirrors were clear at first, but unease prickled. Two blocks from my apartment, a familiar truck tailed me—Kendrick's, jacked up on oversized tires, staying three cars back. He wanted me to see him, hazel eyes locking in the rearview when traffic slowed. The threat moved beyond office walls now, his enforcer loyalty turning stalker. My pulse raced, mental-health sirens blaring—anxiety from months of moral tightrope walking crashing down.

I lost him in a strip mall lot, heart slamming, pulling into my complex garage shaking. Inside my dim apartment, I grabbed the baseball bat from the closet, aluminum cold and reassuring. No lights, no TV—just me by the front door, bat gripped white-knuckled, listening to every creak. Trauma replayed: Ragina's demands, Kendrick's grip, payroll voids. Is he out there? Will he break in? Anxiety reached a fever pitch, sweat beading despite the chill. Felicity's devastated eyes haunted me, Jasper's ramen confession, Lila's alliance. We'd passed the drive, the feds closing in, but personal safety shattered. Sitting there for hours, bat ready, I realized the ghost of payroll was just the start—Ragina's derangement had us all hunted.

Night deepened, shadows lengthening across the floor. Every car door slam outside spiked my pulse, imagination conjuring Kendrick's goatee sneer, his barked threats. I texted the burner group: Kendrick tailed me home. Bat duty. Stay safe.

Felicity: Fuck. Lock doors. Kids asleep—praying.

Jasper: Shit, Em. Pizza was a bad omen. 😄 But seriously, crash here if needed.

Their support anchored me, gritty friendship against the storm. The morally gray path felt grayer—snitching from dirty paychecks, now facing real danger. But justice for the team, for Felicity's mortgage, for Jasper's future, outweighed the fear.

Hours ticked by, the bat heavy in my lap. Anxiety looped: What if he circles back? What if Ragina's keyloggers caught more? Trauma from the fax whirs and the thumb-drive handoff piled on. Profanity-laced thoughts: This bitch's narcissism ends soon. Dawn crept in, no knock, no breach. Exhaustion hit, but sleep evaded me. Kendrick's tail confirmed it—the walls were gone, the threat personal. Tomorrow, more risks, but we'd fight. The ghost of payroll had awakened something fiercer in us, bonds forged in fraud's fire, unbreakable.

By morning light filtering through the blinds, I set the bat down, muscles aching. Coffee brewed, hands still shaky. The group chat buzzed: Survived? Affirmatives rolled in, dark humor masking the mental toll.

Felicity: Mortgage call at 9. Fake it till feds raid.

Jasper: Ramen solidarity. Lila good?

I typed: Drive safe with her lawyer. We're ghosts no more.

Hope stirred amid the grit—Ragina's cards crumbling, our evidence multiplying. But Kendrick's shadow loomed, anxiety a constant companion. This white-collar war had turned visceral, and I was all in.

Vegas or Bust

Saturday morning came too soon after that endless night with the bat by my door. My hands still trembled from the adrenaline crash, but the group chat on our burners lit up with one word: Go. Ragina had texted the office line late Friday, announcing her "business retreat" to Vegas for the weekend. No details, just her usual delusional flair about sealing deals with high-rollers. We knew better. It was another gambling binge, funded by God knows what fresh scam. The moment her leased Bentley peeled out of the lot that morning, tires screeching like her departing sanity, the office atmosphere shifted. Fear evaporated into frantic purpose. We had forty-eight hours to gather everything before she returned, and the feds needed it airtight.

I pulled into the empty parking lot first, my worn messenger bag heavy with the voice recorder and fresh thumb drives. The gloomy gray building looked almost welcoming without her shadow looming. Felicity arrived next in her minivan, sturdy frame emerging with a box of latex gloves and file folders, her tight dark curls in that no-nonsense bun, deep brown eyes flashing determination. Jasper rolled up last in his beat-up truck, his lanky 6'1" frame spilling out with a laptop under one arm and an energy drink in hand, messy sandy hair falling into his twinkling blue eyes. His half-grin was back, freckles bright against his face. "Vegas or bust for the bitch," he quipped, rapid-fire style laced with dark humor. "Let's make it bust for her."

We slipped inside through the back door, hearts pounding but steps light. The office felt like a ghost town, the fluorescent hum the only sound. There were no cameras in the main areas thanks to our earlier sabotage, but we moved fast anyway. "Divide and conquer," I said, voice low and conversational, that gritty realism we'd all leaned into. "Jasper, you're on her cloud storage. Felicity, physical docs from the floorboard. I'll hit the wire logs. Forty-eight hours, people. This is it." Felicity nodded, her stoic powerhouse vibe kicking in, maternal edge softening the tension. "Got it. Kids are with a sitter— double pay for this shit. Let's bury her." Jasper cracked his knuckles, optimistic prankster masking his anxiety. "Hacking time. If I find Vegas nudes, group chat gold."

We scattered like pros. Jasper hunkered down at his desk, laptop whirring as he bypassed Ragina's pathetic password—her dog's birthday, we'd guessed months ago. Felicity pried up the loose floorboard in Ragina's office, the one we'd spotted during a "cleaning" ruse. I dove into the server room, pulling wire-transfer logs from the ancient system she'd refused to upgrade. The air thickened with purpose, our friendship the glue holding this white-collar heist together. Sweat beaded on my forehead, anxiety from Kendrick's tail last night twisting my gut, but focus won out. This was for Felicity's mortgage, Jasper's ramen days, all of us.

Jasper whooped first, breaking the silence. "Holy shit, Em! Felicity! Get in here!" We rushed over, my scuffed flats silent on the carpet. His screen glowed with folders from her private cloud: "Vegas Trips," "Client Deals," "Personal." He clicked into videos, and there she was—Ragina, bottle-blonde hair disheveled in a casino penthouse, hazel eyes wild, designer suit rumpled. She bragged to blurry gambling buddies, voice shrill even through tinny audio. "You shits think I'm broke? I've got wires bigger than your houses! RT Global Holdings washes it all—loans in, clean cash out to my accounts. Fake transfers? Child's play. Do you know who I am?" She laughed maniacally, gold jewelry jangling, waving a stack of forged statements. Self-incriminating gold. Jasper's eyes widened, half-grin gone. "This is it. Feds will cream their pants. She's bragging about scams like it's poker bluffing."

Felicity emerged from Ragina's office, arms loaded with yellowed envelopes and binders. "Floorboard jackpot. Forged invoices, backdated loans, even fake vendor payments. All timestamped wrong—sloppy as her rages." Her voice was direct, no-BS Midwestern clip, profanity bubbling under. "Fuck, this woman's deranged. Look at these notes: 'Blame the team if banks call.'" We piled it on the conference table, a mountain of evidence. My turn. I spread the wire logs, cross-referencing with Jasper's downloads. Patterns emerged fast—funds funneled through "RT Global Holdings," a shell company we'd never heard of. Loans from desperate lenders, laundered clean before hitting her personal accounts for Bentleys and blackjack. "Money laundering," I whispered, introspective grit hitting hard. Morally gray didn't cover this; we'd been complicit by proximity, cashing dirty checks while she partied. Trauma from payroll ghosts and Kendrick's stalk all fueled the fire now.

We worked in sync, a high-stakes race against the clock. Jasper ripped videos to drives, narrating quips to keep spirits up. "Boss lady's got a tell—every bluff ends in 'MY company!'" Felicity sorted docs by crime type, dry wit emerging. "These loans? She can't pay the interest, let alone the principal. My ex was better at hiding booze money." I traced wires, anxiety spiking at every near match. One slip, and we're accessories, my mind raced, hands shaking on the keyboard. Dark comedy threaded through it: Jasper's memes pinged silently on burners, Felicity's maternal eye-rolls at Ragina's handwritten threats. Hours blurred, coffee cold, takeout wrappers piling up. We were doing the work of ten, like old times, but now for justice.

A noise shattered the rhythm—a rattle at the back door. We froze. "Shit," Jasper hissed, voice dropping to a whisper. "Kendrick?" My heart hammered, trauma flashing: his truck tailing me, fists clenched, enforcer loyalty turning predator. Felicity shoved docs under the table, Jasper slammed his laptop shut, screen black. I kicked binders behind chairs, messenger bag zipped tight. The door creaked open. Kendrick lumbered in, his stocky 5'9" build filling the frame, buzzed dark hair damp from rain, hazel eyes narrowing suspiciously under the fluorescents. His company polo stretched over muscles, cargo pants sagging with tools, steel-toed boots thudding. His goatee twitched as he scanned us, coiled energy radiating threat.

"What the fuck are you pussies doing here on a Saturday?" he barked, a gruff, profane growl mixing construction lingo and street slang. His fists clenched unconsciously, a crane tattoo peeking out. We scrambled internally, minds racing for cover. I stepped forward, chestnut bob falling loose, warm brown eyes forcing calm despite my feverish pulse. "Payroll fix," I lied smoothly, conversational grit masking the lie. "Surprise for Ragina. That bank error? We're untangling it before Monday. Loyalty and all." Felicity backed me, sturdy frame straight, practical watch ticking steady. "Yeah. Mortgage won't wait. Figured we'd knock it out." Jasper nodded, playing dumb prankster. "Ramen-fund restoration. Pizza didn't cut it, boss man."

Kendrick stared, a long minute stretching eternal. His eyes darted over the table strewn with "innocent" papers, our flushed faces, the empty lot outside. Suspicion etched his goatee-framed scowl, foster-kid insecurity fueling paranoia. He knows, anxiety screamed, bat-night trauma replaying. Profanity thundered internally: Fuck, don't blow this. He grunted finally, rummaging in his pocket. "Forgot my keys. Ragina'd have my ass." He snatched them from the hook near the door, but as he turned, his phone clattered onto the table— screen lighting up, voice-recorder app open, red dot blinking. Live. He didn't notice, stomping out with a final glare. "Better be fixing shit. Boss finds out you're slacking..." The door slammed, truck revving away.

We exhaled in unison, collapsing against desks. Jasper lunged for the phone, snatching it up. "Holy fuck, it's recording. He left it—on purpose?" Felicity grabbed a drive, copying the audio fast. "Bugging us. Trying to catch whistleblowers. That motherfucker." My hands shook as I grabbed the device. Rewind played his entry, our scramble, my lie—all captured. But we'd caught him too, a digital breadcrumb for the feds. "Twist of the knife," I said, a gritty laugh bubbling with dark comedy. Shell company, videos, now this—Ragina's empire crumbling from within.

We redoubled our efforts, paranoia sharpening focus. Jasper uploaded the recorder audio to the cloud folder, videos syncing. Felicity resealed the floorboard, docs scanned and hidden. I finalized the wire logs, RT Global Holdings exposed in neon detail: loans washed, personal accounts bloated. The mental-health toll hit hard—anxiety knots in my stomach, trauma from the threats layering thick. But team bonds held, morally gray turning righteous. Jasper high-fived me. "Forty-eight hours? We crushed thirty-six." Felicity's eyes softened, fierce maternal pride showing through. "For the kids. For us." We packed out, evidence drives tucked safe, the office wiped clean.

Driving home, the airport distant on the horizon where Ragina partied oblivious, the tension eased fractionally. The group chat buzzed: Videos gold. Shell busted. Kendrick's bug fail. 😄

Felicity: Fuck yeah. Mortgage tomorrow—hope.

Jasper: Vegas bust incoming.

I gripped the wheel, an introspective wave crashing over me. This heist bonded us deeper, white-collar crime's gritty underbelly laid bare. Ragina's narcissism, Kendrick's muscle, all unraveling. Anxiety lingered, but purpose burned brighter. Forty-eight hours down, justice ticking closer.

Back at my apartment, bat stowed but paranoia still high, I reviewed copies on my laptop. The videos looped: her brags, slurred and damning. Shell ledgers mapped the fraud web. The recorder caught Kendrick's suspicion, his accidental bug a gift. Trauma whispered doubts—Will the feds protect us? Is this a setup?—but Felicity's kids, Jasper's grin, our laughter propelled me. Profanity vented silently: Fuck her deranged ass. Sleep came fitfully, dreams of cuffs and casinos. Sunday loomed for polish, but we'd seized the weekend. Vegas or bust? For her, definitely bust.

Monday waited, audit whispers on the horizon, but we'd armed the war. The team was unbreakable, the evidence ironclad. The gloomy gray building held secrets no more; we'd gutted them for light.

The Audit Is Coming

Monday morning hit like a freight train. I pulled into the same gloomy gray parking lot with that familiar knot in my stomach, the weight of the weekend's evidence haul pressing down on me. The office building loomed, its windows reflecting a sky heavy with clouds that matched my mood. Jasper, Felicity, and I had nailed the raid on Ragina's secrets, but now reality crashed back. Her Bentley was already there, gleaming unnaturally under the lot lights. She was back from Vegas early, and something told me it wasn't with pockets full of winnings. The group chat on our burners buzzed softly in my pocket:

Jasper: Showtime. Stay frosty.

Felicity: Kids fed. Let's survive this shit.

I grabbed my messenger bag, hands steady for once, and headed in.

The office hummed with tension thicker than usual. Jasper sat at his desk, lanky frame hunched over his keyboard, pretending to crunch numbers while his blue eyes darted. Felicity moved like a machine in the admin corner, her sturdy build efficient, curls tight in that bun, sorting files with a stoic focus that hid her exhaustion. Her single-mom strength shone through as she balanced a coffee and a stack of invoices. We exchanged quick nods, our friendship the only anchor in this storm. Then the conference room door flew open, and Ragina stormed out, her bottle-blonde hair a mess, hazel eyes bloodshot and wild. Her designer suit hung loose, like she'd lost weight at the tables or just her grip on reality. She looked hungover, frantic, jangling gold jewelry clashing with her talons tapping furiously.

"Emily! Get your ass in here now!" Her voice cracked like a whip, shrill and demanding, echoing off the gray walls. The office froze. Jasper's half-grin faltered, Felicity's jaw tightened. I felt every eye on me as I stood, chestnut bob falling loose, warm brown eyes masking the anxiety twisting my gut. This is it, I thought, the morally gray area we'd danced in all weekend turning pitch black. Ragina had lost big again—I could smell the desperation, the profanity-laced rage brewing. I walked into her office, the door slamming behind me like a trap snapping shut.

Her space was chaos: empty champagne bottles from Vegas shoved in the trash, papers strewn like confetti from a bad party. She paced, her 5'10" frame imposing even in defeat, makeup smudged under those piercing eyes. "Sit," she barked, thrusting a thick stack of blank bank stationery and a laser-printer cartridge at me.

My hands took them automatically, heart pounding. "A major lender is sending a forensic auditor. Wednesday. Some nosy fuck sniffing around our loans." She leaned in close, breath sour with booze and defeat. "I've lost another fifty grand in Vegas—those bastards rigged the tables, but that's beside the point.

This is my company, Emily. You create a year's worth of profitable statements. Make it look good. Wires in, profits out. Test of loyalty."

I stared at the paper, the printer, the forgery kit laid bare. My mind raced back to the weekend—RT Global Holdings, her brags on video, Kendrick's bugged phone. This was the smoking gun we'd prayed for, but now it was in my lap. "Ragina, that's... that's forging documents," I said, voice conversational but gritty, buying time. Anxiety clawed up my throat, trauma from her past rages flashing: thrown staplers, screamed threats. She laughed, a manic sound that chilled me. "Forging? It's survival, you little shit. Do this, and a ten-grand bonus is yours. Cash. No taxes. But fuck it up, and I'll destroy you. References? Gone. Your name blackened. Everyone knows you're against me because I'm a woman clawing my way up."

The weight hit hard. If I did it, I was a criminal, complicit in wire fraud, money laundering—years in a cell next to her. If I refused, she'd unleash hell: calls to my old bosses, smears online, maybe worse with Kendrick lurking. Morally gray didn't cut it; this was abyss-black. I nodded slowly, playing the loyal drone. "Okay. I'll handle it." She grinned, victim act flipping on. "Good girl. Don't make me regret trusting you." I left her office, the stack heavy in my arms, my hands already starting to shake. The team caught my eye—Jasper mouthed, What the fuck? Felicity's deep brown eyes radiated quiet strength, but worry creased her face. We were in deep now.

I needed air, guidance—now. Lunch break hit, and I slipped out to the local diner down the block, a greasy spoon with vinyl booths and the smell of fries cutting through my nausea. My contact from the DA's office waited in the back, a no-nonsense guy named Detective

Ruiz, mid-forties with a salt-and-pepper beard and eyes that saw through bullshit. He slid into the booth across from me, coffee black, voice low. "Talk." I spilled it all—the audit bombshell, Ragina's hungover return, the fifty-grand Vegas loss she admitted in rage, the direct order to forge statements. "Blank stationery, printer. A year's worth. Bonus bait, loyalty test. She's cornered."

Ruiz nodded, unflappable, but his fingers drummed the table. "This is gold, Harris. Perfect timing. We need you to stay undercover. Comply just enough—get the auditor in the door Wednesday. But don't actually break the law. Sabotage it subtly. Easter eggs only a forensic guy spots: wrong MICR lines, mismatched hashes, timestamps off by seconds. We want her handing them over, thinking she's safe." I leaned in, voice dropping to a whisper, anxiety spilling out. "And me? If she sniffs it, I'm the fall guy. Forgery in my hands, my prints on the printer. I'm terrified I'm being set up here, Detective. This morally gray shit—it's crushing me. Trauma from her threats, Kendrick's stalking... what if it goes south?"

He met my eyes, steady. "You're not alone. Whistleblower protections kick in once you deliver. We've got the shell-company docs, videos, Kendrick's recorder—it's airtight. But we need this audit to trigger the raid. Stay the course. Pressure's on, but you're the key." Profanity bubbled up, my gritty realism cracking. "Fuck, this is insane. My hands are shaking just thinking about printing those lies." He clapped my shoulder, rare warmth in the gesture. "Anxiety's normal. You've got the team, and you've got us. Eat something." I forced down fries, stomach churning, but purpose hardened. Back to the office, or the ship sank without me.

The conference room became my war zone that afternoon. I set up the laser printer on the table, the stack of blank sheets mocking me. Jasper hovered first, lanky frame leaning in, freckles bright with worry. "Em, that's felony-level shit. What'd she say?" I filled him in low, his rapid-fire quips dying into a serious nod. "Sabotage it, then. Make her own noose." Felicity joined us, sturdy mom jeans swishing, practical watch ticking like a bomb. "I've got your back. Kids need a world without her kind." Their friendship fueled me, dark comedy threading in—Jasper's meme about "printing money, literally 😂"—but tension gripped tight. Ragina paced outside the glass walls, glancing in, paranoia in every jangle.

I started the work, fingers flying on the ancient accounting software we'd jury-rigged for her scams before. I pulled real templates, fudged numbers to show profits where debts hid: wires from RT Global Holdings inflated, loans "repaid," casino cash disguised as client payments. But the sabotage—oh, I wove it carefully. MICR lines off by a digit, routing numbers swapped with ghosts from defunct banks. Hash values mismatched, digital fingerprints screaming fake to any auditor worth his salt. Timestamps forward-dated by seconds, tying back to her Vegas flight logs we'd fed the DA. She's done, I thought, but my hands shook violently as the printer whirred, spitting out lies page by page. Ink gleamed false, each sheet a step deeper into the gray. Sweat beaded on my forehead, anxiety peaking—what if the errors were too subtle? Too obvious? Ragina burst in midway, talons landing on my shoulder. "Faster! Make it perfect. That bonus is yours if it fools him."

"Almost there," I lied, voice steady through gritted teeth. She ranted about Vegas cheats, sexist lenders, her sacrifices. "They think they can audit me? I've built this from nothing!" I nodded, introspective hell raging inside: We've cashed her dirty checks for months. Am I any better? Felicity slipped in with coffee, her dry wit a lifeline. "Don't let her see you sweat. We've got the evidence mountain." Jasper manned lookout, deflecting Kendrick's prowls—stocky enforcer lurking, eyes suspicious post-weekend. The printer hummed on, the stack growing to a foot high. Two hundred pages of doom, errors embedded like mines. My trauma surfaced in flashes—nights with the bat, payroll fears—but resolve steeled. This was white-collar warfare, our friendship the weapon.

Hours blurred, the sun dipping low. Ragina snatched the final stack, flipping through it with greedy eyes. "Beautiful. Loyalty pays, Emily." She vanished to her office, bonus promise hanging in the air. I collapsed into a chair, hands still trembling, the act of printing lies etched into my palms. Jasper high-fived me tentatively. "Easter eggs deployed. Auditor's Christmas." Felicity hugged me quickly, maternal strength bolstering mine. "Proud of you. Fuck her games." The group chat lit up: We did it. Hands off now. But paranoia gnawed— Kendrick's glare from the hall, Ragina's wild eyes. The audit loomed Wednesday, our sabotage the trigger. Anxiety knotted deep, morally gray turning to steel resolve. We'd survive this, expose her deranged empire.

The gloomy gray building held its breath, justice ticking closer.

Driving home that night, city lights blurring, I replayed it all. Vegas losses, the forgery order, DA pressure—each piece locked into place. My hands steadied on the wheel, but the mental-health toll weighed heavy: sleepless nights ahead, trauma layering with anxiety. Yet the team's bond, that office friendship born in hell, kept me going. Ragina thought she owned us; what she really owned was her downfall. Wednesday would crack the facade, cuffs waiting. Dark comedy whispered in my head: Print your own ticket to prison, boss. Purpose burned brighter than fear.

Amanda Ray

The Glass Floor

Wednesday morning arrived with a tension that hung in the air like smoke from a smoldering fire. I pulled into the parking lot of that same gloomy gray building, heart pounding harder than ever before. The forged files sat heavy in my messenger bag, those sabotaged statements I had printed just days ago, riddled with the tiny errors that would unravel everything. Jasper and Felicity were already there, their cars parked close together like a silent show of solidarity. We had exchanged quick texts in our burner group chat last night, steeling ourselves for the auditor's arrival. Ragina's Bentley gleamed mockingly in its spot, and I knew she was inside, probably pacing her office with that manic energy she got when cornered.

The office felt like a pressure cooker from the moment I stepped through the door. Jasper looked up from his desk, his lanky frame slouched but his blue eyes sharp with mischief masking real anxiety. "Morning, boss lady," he quipped softly, his voice in that rapid-fire tone laced with dark humor. "Auditor day's here. Think Ragina's charm offensive will work?" Felicity, sturdy and unflappable in her mom jeans and sensible blouse, gave a tight nod from her admin station, her deep brown eyes radiating that quiet strength. "Just get through it," she muttered, her Midwestern clip direct and no-BS. "Kids are counting on us not fucking this up." I forced a smile, my chestnut bob tied back hastily, warm brown eyes shadowed by the weight of what was coming. The friendship we had built in this hellhole was the only thing keeping me from bolting.

Then the front door opened, and in walked Mr. Henderson, the stone-faced auditor. He was in his late fifties, tall and lean with a severe crew cut and wire-rimmed glasses that made his gray eyes look even colder. He carried a slim leather briefcase, dressed in a crisp navy suit that screamed no-nonsense professionalism. Ragina swooped in like a predator scenting prey, her bottle-blonde hair teased high, designer suit straining at the seams, gold jewelry jangling. She flipped her switch to saccharine charm, all smiles and fluttering lashes. "Mr. Henderson! Welcome to RT Construction. I'm Ragina Thomas, the visionary behind it all. Let me get you something to ease that long drive."

She led him straight to the conference room, our glass-walled fishbowl where everything was on display. I watched as she poured him a glass of expensive scotch from the bottle she kept hidden in her office credenza, the kind that cost more than our monthly paychecks. "To growth and prosperity," she toasted, her voice dripping honey, talking animatedly about her grand "vision" for expanding into commercial high-rises and luxury developments. Henderson accepted the drink with a polite nod, but his expression never softened, those stone-gray eyes scanning the room like he was already tallying discrepancies. Ragina laughed too loudly, touching his arm lightly, but he shrugged it off subtly, focusing on his briefcase.

"Emily!" Ragina called sharply, snapping her fingers. "Bring in the financials. Our office manager here has everything prepared." My stomach twisted into knots, anxiety spiking as I grabbed the stack of sabotaged files from my desk. This was the moment—the handoff of the poison pills I had crafted under her orders, those fake statements with mismatched hashes and off timestamps that any forensic expert would spot. I walked into the conference room, the glass walls making me feel exposed, every eye in the office on me. Jasper shot me a thumbs-up from his desk, Felicity's gaze steady with support. I placed the thick binder on the table before Henderson, my hands steady despite the internal storm. "Here are the statements for the past year, sir," I said, voice even.

Henderson opened the binder without a word, his stone face unchanging as he flipped through pages, pulling out a loupe to examine the print quality. Ragina hovered, still in charm mode, rambling about client wins and aggressive bidding strategies that never happened. "We've got big things coming, Mr. Henderson. Loans repaid, wires flowing—RT is unstoppable." He grunted noncommittally, marking notes on a yellow legal pad. I lingered by the glass wall, pretending to organize, watching his every move. The errors were there, buried but glaring to his trained eye: MICR lines wrong, routing numbers tied to phantom accounts and her shell companies. My mind raced with what-ifs—what if he missed them? What if Ragina saw my hesitation?

That's when Kendrick cornered me. He materialized from the hallway, his stocky 5'9" build blocking my path to the copy machine, buzzed hair and goatee sharp, hazel eyes narrowed with that coiled aggression. His company polo stretched over his muscles, cargo pants stuffed with tools. "Emily, we need to talk. Now." His voice was gruff, barked low like an order, profanity edging in. "Outside.

Truck." I glanced at the conference room—Ragina was still schmoozing, Henderson buried in files—and nodded, heart hammering. Anxiety clawed at me; this bully had menaced us for months, intimidating subs, throwing his weight around. But something in his narrowed eyes looked off—not just threat, but desperation.

We slipped out to the parking lot, the gloomy gray building looming behind us. Kendrick led me to his beat-up F-150 truck, the one with the crane-tattoo sticker on the bumper, climbing into the driver's seat and gesturing for me to get in. The cab smelled of stale energy drinks and motor oil, his fists clenching the wheel unconsciously. "I know what you're doing," he started, voice rough, street slang mixing with construction lingo. "Feeding shit to the cops. Those recordings, the shell docs. I've seen you sneaking calls, deleting files." My blood ran cold, trauma flashing from his past threats— shoving vendors, yelling at us over bounced checks. "Fuck, Kendrick, if you're here to threaten—"

He cut me off, leaning in close, his breath hot. "No, listen. I've been protecting your ass from her worst impulses. Ragina's deranged, Emily. Paranoid as fuck. She's had me intimidating subs, strong-arming them for partial payments, fudging site reports. Forced me, you know? 'Do it or you're out.' But I've got my own secret recordings—her ordering me to scare Lila Hargrove's crew, threatening to blacklist them unless they took IOUs. Voice memos on my phone, timestamps matching her rages."

I stared, morally gray twisting deeper. This was the enforcer, the bully who enjoyed his power trips, now flipping? "Why tell me? You could've gone to the feds yourself." He laughed bitterly, a mocking sound. "Scared shitless. Prison for extortion if I don't cut a deal. But you—you're the one with the DA contact. Trade my evidence for immunity. We both walk, testify against her. She's sinking, Emily. Ship's going down. Protect me like I've protected you." His hazel eyes darted, revealing fear beneath the macho facade—foster-kid trauma peeking through, terror of abandonment. I didn't trust him fully; he was a thug who'd relished the power. But his recordings could seal the case. "I'll... think about it," I said, voice gritty, buying time. Anxiety gnawed—was this a trap?

We headed back inside, whispering low as we re-entered the office. That's when Ragina exploded. She had caught sight of us through the glass walls, her piercing hazel eyes blazing from the conference room. She burst out, talons pointing, bottle-blonde hair flying wild. "What the fuck is this? You two sneaking around like rats? Having a goddamn affair to steal my company?" Her voice rose to a shrill scream, echoing through the open office, profanity flying. Jasper froze mid-keystroke, Felicity's jaw dropped. Henderson looked up impassively from his files.

"Ragina, it's not—" I started, but she cut me off, turning on Kendrick with volcanic rage. "You! My enforcer, my loyal guy, fucking the office manager behind my back? You're fired! Get your shit and get out! This is MY company!" She hurled a stapler at him, missing but clattering across the floor. Kendrick's face reddened, fists clenching, but he held back—for once. "You're crazy,

Ragina. Paranoid bitch," he growled, grabbing his jacket. The office was dead silent, tension gritty and thick. He stormed out, slamming the door, but paused at his truck in the lot, yelling through the open window so I could hear: "The ship's sinking, Emily! She's the only one left on deck!" Then his tires screeched as he peeled away.

Ragina turned on me, jabbing a manicured talon inches from my face. "Don't think I don't see you, Emily. Plotting with him. Loyalty test failed. But you're staying—someone has to clean this mess." Her eyes darted suspiciously, makeup cracking under sweat, the facade slipping. Henderson cleared his throat from the conference room. "Ms. Thomas, if you're done? I'd like the digital originals next." She spun, charm flickering back weakly. "Of course! Emily, get them." But her public meltdown had cracked something—staff whispering, Jasper texting furiously in our chat:

Holy shit, enforcer down. You're exposed.

I nodded, pulse racing, realizing the shift. Kendrick was gone, potentially flipping with his evidence. Ragina's jealousy and rage had fired her own muscle, leaving me as the last target of her spiraling paranoia. The glass walls felt like a trap now, her hazel eyes tracking my every move. Felicity slipped me a note: Stay strong. We've got you. Jasper's half-grin returned faintly, a dark-comedy nod to the chaos. But inside, anxiety churned with trauma—months of threats, forged docs, morally gray turning blacker. Henderson's audit was underway, my sabotage ticking like a bomb. Ragina thought she controlled the narrative, but the floor beneath her was glass, cracking under the weight of her delusions.

As Henderson delved deeper into the files, marking more notes, I retreated to my desk, mind whirling. Kendrick's offer echoed—trade for immunity, his recordings of her ordering intimidation. Lila Hargrove's unpaid crew, the bounced checks he'd enforced. It could bury her deeper in extortion charges. But trusting a bully? His fear of Ragina had seemed real, that gruff voice cracking with foster-kid vulnerability. Still, morally gray didn't begin to cover it; he was complicit, enjoyed the power. My hands shook recalling his past rages, the way he'd loomed over Felicity once, profanity barking. Yet desperation made strange allies in white-collar crime wars.

Ragina retreated to her office post-meltdown, slamming the door, but not before hissing at me, "Watch yourself, Emily. Everyone's against me because I'm a woman building an empire." Her victim act, delusional boasts—classic. The office buzzed with stunned chatter; Jasper leaned over. "Dude just flipped the script. You okay?" His voice quippy but eyes serious, freckles standing out against pale worry. "Anxiety's through the roof," I admitted low, gritty realism spilling out. "He's got evidence, but what if it's a setup? And now I'm her sole target." Felicity joined us, maternal edge firm. "Fuck him if he betrays. We've got the feds. Survive the day."

Henderson called for more docs, his stone face finally cracking into a faint frown at a mismatched timestamp. Progress. Ragina peeked from her door, paranoia radiating. My friendship with Jasper and Felicity anchored me—their dry wit, unyielding support amid the grit. Dark comedy threaded through Jasper's whisper:

"Enforcer yeeted. Next up, boss in cuffs?" I laughed shakily, but reality bit: I was on deck alone now, waves crashing. The mental-health toll mounted—sleepless nights, trauma layering—but justice burned brighter. The audit rolled on, Ragina's empire teetering on that glass floor, ready to shatter.

By afternoon, Henderson had a stack of flagged pages, his legal pad filled. Ragina hovered, scotch glass refilled, charm fraying. "Everything's in order, right?" she pressed. He ignored her, packing up methodically. "I'll need digital access tomorrow," he said flatly. She nodded too eagerly, eyes darting to me accusingly. Kendrick's truck was long gone, his yell echoing in my head. I was the primary target now—paranoia aimed squarely at me. But with his potential flip, the noose tightened on her, not us. The tension stayed gritty and serious, the crime web unraveling thread by thread.

Amanda Ray

Cameras Everywhere

Thursday dawned with a heaviness that pressed down on me like the humid air before a storm. I pulled into the parking lot of that same gloomy gray building, my hands gripping the steering wheel a little too tight. Kendrick was gone, fired in that explosive meltdown yesterday, and now Ragina's paranoia had zeroed in on me. The auditor, Mr. Henderson, had requested the original digital files today, not those sabotaged printouts. This was it, the moment of truth where the real data would either bury her or blow up in our faces. Jasper and Felicity were already there, their cars side by side, a small beacon of our friendship in this mess. Our group chat had been blowing up all night with anxious texts and dark jokes to keep the anxiety at bay.

I stepped inside, the office feeling smaller, more claustrophobic than ever. Jasper looked up from his desk, his messy sandy hair falling into his eyes, that half-grin masking the tension. "Morning, Em. Survived the night?" he asked, his voice light but his blue eyes serious. Felicity nodded from her station, her tight dark curls in a bun, deep brown eyes steady. "Ragina's been in early. Something's off," she said in her direct, no-BS tone. I forced a smile, settling at my desk, my chestnut bob tied back, worry lines etched deeper on my forehead. The mental weight of the past months—the forged wires, the threats, the morally gray areas we navigated—it all churned inside me, trauma layering on like sediment.

That's when I noticed them. Cameras. New ones, high-tech black domes gleaming from every corner: over desks, in hallways, even staring down from the bathroom doors. Ragina had lost it completely without Kendrick to rein her in. Her behavior was erratic, unhinged. She'd spent thousands—money we didn't have—on this surveillance nightmare. I glanced toward her office, the door ajar, and there she was, perched like a vulture behind a wall of monitors, her bottle-blonde hair teased high, hazel eyes darting across screens. She tracked every move, every blink. The psychological weight hit me hard; I felt exposed, violated, anxiety spiking as I imagined her watching me pee.

"Emily," her voice crackled over the intercom, shrill and demanding. "I see you just sat down. Get coffee for Henderson. He's due any minute." I froze, my heart pounding. How long had she been monitoring? I stood slowly, grabbing a mug, the camera above my desk whirring faintly as it followed. Felicity shot me a look, her maternal edge showing in the tight set of her jaw. "This is fucked," she muttered low, profanity slipping out for emphasis. Jasper nodded, freckles standing out on his pale face. "Cameras in the shitter? That's next-level deranged." Dark comedy threaded through his words, but the grit was real. We were rats in her maze now.

Henderson arrived promptly, his severe crew cut and wire-rimmed glasses unchanged, briefcase in hand. Ragina swept out, charm dialed up but fraying at the edges, her designer suit straining, gold jewelry jangling. "Mr. Henderson, right this way. Emily has your coffee." She glanced at a monitor, eyes narrowing on me. He nodded curtly, settling in the glass conference room again. "Ms. Harris," he said flatly, "I'll need the original digital files now. Not printouts. Server access or drives." My stomach twisted. This was the pivot. The fakes Ragina had approved were riddled with errors, but the originals—the real ones with every forged wire, shell company transfer, unpaid loan—those would end her.

I nodded, throat dry. "Of course, sir. I'll pull them from the server." Ragina's eyes locked on her central monitor from her office, fixed on my hands as I approached my desk. She thought I was handing over the doctored drives, the ones she'd forced us to fake. But Jasper and I had prepped the real ones hidden in the server room, ready for the swap. Her paranoia had her glued to the screens, talons tapping impatiently. "Hurry up, Emily," she snapped over the intercom. "Don't think I don't see you dragging your feet. Everyone's out to get me because I'm a strong woman running this empire."

The weight of her gaze through the cameras was crushing. I couldn't just walk to the server room; she'd spot it instantly. Anxiety clawed at me, trauma from her rages flashing—screaming fits, thrown staplers, accusations of affairs. Morally gray didn't cover it anymore; this was survival. I texted Jasper under the desk: Need diversion. Now. His phone buzzed, and he grinned faintly, standing with purpose. "Hey, Felicity, microwave that popcorn I brought? Movie-night vibes to beat the tension." She rolled her eyes but handed him a bag from the break-room stash.

Ragina's voice boomed again. "Emily, what's taking so long? Henderson's waiting!" Her eyes bored into the screen, every pixel of my movements scrutinized. I edged toward the server room door, heart hammering, but the cameras covered it too. Jasper positioned himself by the kitchenette microwave, visible on her monitors. He punched in the max time, the bag bulging, smoke starting to curl. "Oops," he muttered loud enough for the mics, that boyish mischief in play. The bag ignited, acrid smoke billowing fast, the fire alarm shrieking seconds later. Chaos erupted.

People jumped up, coughing, alarms blaring. Henderson stood calmly in the conference room, but Ragina exploded from her office, coughing and screaming profanities. "What the fuck is this? Fire? Sabotage! Everyone out!" Smoke filled the air, thick and popcorn-scented, triggering sprinklers in spots. Jasper waved dramatically. "My bad! Popcorn apocalypse!" His risk was huge—job on the line—but his loyalty to our friendship, to justice, shone through. In the pandemonium, eyes watering, I slipped into the server room unnoticed, the door clicking shut behind me.

The room hummed with fans, racks of drives blinking in the dim light. My hands shook as I yanked the fake drive—the one Ragina's ops cronies had prepped with scrubbed data—and slotted in the real one, packed with evidence: fake wires timestamped to her vacations, shell loans to gambling dens disguised as vendors, bounced checks to subs like Lila Hargrove. Every incriminating byte. I wiped it down, heart racing, anxiety peaking. What if she checks right away? What if Jasper's caught? Trauma from months of this—watching her ruin lives, strong-arm subs, blame us for her delusions—fueled me.

I emerged into the smoke just as Felicity herded everyone toward the exit, her stoic strength a rock.

The fire department showed up quickly, fans clearing the air. Ragina was furious, stalking the lot, yelling into her phone about lawsuits, her makeup smudged, hair deflated. "That little shit Jasper! Popcorn? In my office? He's gone too!" But Jasper played dumb, freckled face innocent. "Accident, boss. Won't happen again." She eyed him suspiciously but turned as Henderson emerged, coughing lightly. "Ms. Thomas, perhaps we resume tomorrow? This is... disruptive." She nodded, seething, missing the swap entirely.

Back inside, alarms silenced, the office reeked of burnt popcorn. Ragina retreated to her monitors, barking at me over the intercom. "Emily, get Henderson the drive. And make it quick. I saw everything—you were slow." Her eyes fixed on the screen again, but triumph gleamed; she thought the fake was in play. I handed Henderson the real drive in the conference room, his gray eyes flickering with something like approval. "This will do," he said, pocketing it. Ragina watched from afar, smiling smugly, convinced she'd won.

I returned to my desk, a cold sense of triumph washing over me. The data swap worked. Jasper high-fived me discreetly, Felicity slipping me a note: Proud of you. Fuck her. But the cameras loomed, her voice crackling again. "Emily, bathroom break? Two minutes. That's suspicious." Psychological warfare, pure and simple. I couldn't even piss without commentary. The mental-health toll was brutal—anxiety constant, trauma from her invasive hell building. Morally gray? We'd crossed into gray heroism, risking it all for the team, for justice.

Later, as Henderson left with the drive, Ragina called me in. Her office was a shrine to delusion: framed fake awards, monitors showing frozen feeds of us working. "You see that, Emily? Everyone plotting. But I won today. Auditor has my clean files. They'll see RT's golden." She laughed, shrill, pouring scotch. Up close, her hazel eyes darted, paranoia etched deep. "Kendrick was weak, but you're loyal, right? Or are you fucking him too?" Profanity laced her victim rant. I nodded mutely, grit holding me. Enjoy it while it lasts, I thought. The explosion was coming, the feds closing in with the real data.

The day dragged, cameras whirring relentlessly. At lunch break, I hit the bathroom, feeling her eyes even there. "One minute forty-five," she intercommed as I exited. Jasper texted: Diversion gold star. Your turn next time? 😂 Dark comedy kept us sane. Felicity pulled me aside. "I've got stretch marks from stress-eating her bullshit, but we're almost free." Her voice was maternal, with a profane edge cutting through. Our friendship was the lifeline in this white-collar nightmare.

By quitting time, Ragina lounged behind her screens, sipping scotch, oblivious. "Good work today, team. Despite the sabotage." She thought she'd tricked the auditor, her empire safe. I packed up, triumph cold and sharp, but anxiety lingered. Cameras everywhere, her erratic rages unbound without Kendrick. The server swap was flawless, Jasper's risk paying off. As I drove away, the gloomy building shrinking in the rearview, I knew the raid loomed. Her delusions would shatter soon, and we'd watch from afar. But for now, the psychological weight pressed on, trauma raw, morally gray paths leading to light.

That night, the group chat lit up.

Jasper: "Popcorn hero reporting. No firing... yet."

Felicity: "Kids say thanks for not fucking up dinner with overtime."

Me: "Swap done. Real data with Henderson. She's clueless."

Dark laughs amid the grit, our bond unbreakable. Ragina's surveillance state had backfired; her obsession blinded her to the real threat. Triumph felt earned, hard-won after months of anxiety, profanity-laced vents, and mental-health strain. The crime web tightened, her end near.

Reflecting in bed, insomnia gripping me, I replayed it all. The cameras' cold stare, her intercom jabs, Jasper's burnt-bag diversion—pure genius under pressure. His arc from jokester to ally shone through, risking his fresh career for us. Felicity's quiet power, my introspective grit pushing through trauma. Ragina's narcissism fueled her fall, installing bathroom cameras in manic fury, spending phantom money on monitors to watch phantoms conspire. White-collar crime at its deranged peak. Cold triumph settled deeper. The explosion was imminent.

The Identity Thief

Friday morning hit me like a freight train, the kind that rattles your bones long after it passes. I had barely slept, my mind replaying the popcorn chaos from yesterday, the server swap, Ragina's smug victory lap over her monitors. The cameras were still there, watching every twitch, but now the real data was out, with Henderson, with the feds. I dragged myself to my car, the gloomy gray building looming in the distance like a bad dream I couldn't shake. My phone buzzed as I pulled into the lot—Jasper and Felicity were already parked, their cars a silent show of solidarity. But it wasn't a group-chat ping. It was my bank.

"Ms. Harris? This is Teller Ramirez from First National Branch on Elm. We need to verify a withdrawal attempt on your savings account." The voice was calm, professional, but my gut twisted instantly. "Someone tried to pull ten thousand dollars using your Social Security number and a forged ID. We flagged it, but can you come in?" I gripped the phone, heart slamming. "Describe the person," I said, voice barely steady. She paused. "Tall woman, late forties maybe, bottle-blonde hair, heavy makeup, designer suit—looked out of place for our branch. Hazel eyes, lots of gold jewelry." It was her. Ragina. My boss, the deranged queen of RT Construction, had crossed from corporate fraud into straight-up personal theft. Rage boiled up, hot and uncontrollable, mixing with the anxiety that had been my constant shadow for months.

I sat in my car for a minute, breathing hard, the trauma of the last six months crashing over me—the forged wires, the threats, the moral tightrope we'd walked. This wasn't just white-collar bullshit anymore; this was my life she was trying to steal. I texted the group quickly: Bank called. Ragina tried to drain my savings. 10K. Using my SSN. Holy fuck. Jasper replied instantly: That psycho bitch. Feds know? Felicity: Drive safe. We're here. I needed to report this, to make it official. But first, the bank branch to confirm, sign whatever they needed. The drive there felt endless, my mind racing with scenarios—her talons flashing that fake ID, smirking at the teller, thinking she'd hit the jackpot on my modest savings.

At the bank, Teller Ramirez met me at the counter, her face sympathetic. She pulled up the security footage on a back terminal, and there she was: Ragina, imposing in her too-tight power suit, hair teased to the heavens, jangling gold as she slid over the forged ID. My photo, my details, but her face glaring back. "She got mad when we stalled, said it was urgent business funds," Ramirez said. "We called security discreetly." I nodded, signing the fraud report, my hands shaking. Ten grand. My emergency fund, my safety net after years of scraping by. The profanity bubbled in my throat—fucking monster—but I kept it in, the gritty realism of it all sinking in. This woman blamed us for her empty accounts, spent phantom money on cameras and scotch, and now targeted me directly. Identity theft, the ultimate violation.

From there, I went straight to the police station. The desk sergeant took my statement, eyes widening at the RT Construction connection. "This the same Ragina Thomas we've been hearing about from the DA's office?" he asked. I nodded, spilling the context—the fraud investigation, the tips we'd fed anonymously for months. He led me to a conference room where DA Investigator Hale—same last name as Jasper, weird coincidence—waited. Mid-forties, sharp suit, no-nonsense vibe. "Emily, sit. We saw your bank's alert cross our desk." He leaned forward. "It's her, no doubt. But hold off filing formally."

"What? She tried to bankrupt me!" My voice cracked, rage spilling out. The anxiety hit its peak, trauma flashing—her screams, thrown objects, the constant paranoia wearing us down like acid. Hale held up a hand. "I get it. Believe me. But the raid's tomorrow morning, nine sharp. FBI's lead now, with Henderson's real data sealing it. Wire fraud, money laundering, forgery—the works. If you file now, she bolts or tips off her ops cronies. We need her in the office, complacent. One more day, Emily. Then cuffs."

One more day. Sitting across from the woman who had just tried to gut my financial life. The morally gray line blurred again—endure abuse for the bigger win, protect the team, nail her completely. I swallowed hard. "Fine. But if she pulls anything else—" Hale nodded. "You've been gold with the tips. Whistleblower protections kick in post-raid. Go to work, act normal. Watch her squirm tomorrow." I left the station shaking, the weight of it all pressing down. Dark comedy flickered—Ragina the Identity Thief, coming to theaters near a federal pen—but the grit overpowered it. My face felt etched with lines that weren't there months ago, stress aging me overnight.

Back at RT Construction, the gloomy gray facade mocked me. Jasper and Felicity were at their desks, shooting me worried looks as I walked in. Cameras whirred overhead, Ragina's eyes somewhere behind those lenses. She swept out of her office mid-morning, lunch in hand—a lavish spread from that overpriced deli downtown, lobster roll and truffle fries, no doubt charged to a fake company card. "Emily, darling, join me? Celebrate our audit win!" Her voice dripped saccharine, hazel eyes darting suspiciously, but smug. She thought the fake drive had fooled everyone.

I forced a smile, rage churning inside like a storm. "Sure, boss." We sat at the conference table, her munching away, jewelry jangling. "You know, Emily, some people are jealous of strong women like me. But you? You're loyal." She winked, biting into her lunch, knowing nothing of the bank fiasco. Or did she? The thought spiked my anxiety—had she seen me leave early? Cameras everywhere. I picked at a stale granola bar I'd brought, watching her spend stolen money right in front of me. You fucking thief, I thought, fists clenched under the table. Uncontrollable fury bubbled, trauma from her rages, her delusions, now personal. But I played it cool, nodding along to her boasts about "protecting the family."

Jasper texted discreetly: She's got balls trying to rob u then lunching like a queen. Hang in. I excused myself, heading to the break room for air. Felicity was there, nursing coffee, her sturdy frame slumped, dark curls escaping her bun. Stretch marks peeked from her sleeves, badges from single-mom battles now amplified by this hell. "Em," she said, voice low and direct, Midwestern clip edged with profanity. "You okay? Group chat lit."

I collapsed into a chair, the dam breaking. "Bank called. Ragina used my SSN, fake ID, tried for ten K from my savings. Feds say wait—one more day." Her deep brown eyes widened, then hardened. "Fuck. That explains her good mood." She paused, gripping her mug. "Mine too, Em. Months ago. Credit trashed, bankruptcy filing I didn't authorize. Debts in my name—loans she couldn't pay, shell companies. My kids' future? Fucked because of her." Her voice cracked, stoic facade slipping, revealing the bottled anxiety, the maternal terror.

We sat there, two women broken by the same monster. Her practical blouse rumpled, my ponytail frayed, faces etched with trauma—worry lines, shadows under our eyes from sleepless nights dodging her schemes. "I've been fighting it quietly," Felicity continued, "lawyers, credit freezes. But her? She blamed me for 'loose paperwork.' I've got two kids counting on that paycheck, but fuck if I'm going down with her sinking ship." Profanity punctuated her pain, her dry wit absent now. I reached over, squeezing her hand. "She's done tomorrow. Real data's out, your bankruptcy's evidence too."

The shared trauma bonded us deeper, our friendship the only light in this white-collar nightmare. Anxiety thrummed—what if she tries again? What if the raid flops? Morally gray choices haunted me: staying silent on my theft to ensure hers. But justice loomed. "Henderson's drive? It had those loan docs timestamped to her Vegas trips," Felicity said, fierce now. "Cops have them. We're almost free." We hugged quickly, her strength maternal, mine gritty resolve. Dark comedy crept back—identity thieves united against the queen bitch—but the grit dominated, the mental-health toll raw.

Ragina paged me over the intercom mid-afternoon. "Emily, my office. Now." Cameras followed as I walked in, her space reeking of scotch and delusion—monitors flickering with our feeds, fake awards gleaming. She lounged, feet up, still picking at lunch remnants. "Everything good? You seem off." Her eyes narrowed, talons tapping. Fury surged—I wanted to scream about the bank, the theft—but Hale's words held me back. "Just tired, boss. Long week." She laughed, shrill. "Cameras don't lie. You and Felicity whispering? Loyal girls stick together." Gloating, oblivious. I nodded, hiding the rage, watching her sip from a crystal glass, living large on fraud.

The day dragged, tension building organically. Jasper diverted with dad jokes over IM—"Why'd Ragina steal your ID? Bad hair day on hers?"—keeping sanity afloat. But break-room chats with Felicity lingered in my mind, her bankruptcy story fueling my fire. We'd endured illegal orders, surveillance hell, and now personal ruin. Trauma ran deep: panic attacks hushed in stalls, anxiety dreams of bounced checks, moral quandaries over cashing dirty pay. Strong language vented in chats: This cunt's end can't come soon enough.

Quitting time neared, Ragina still gloating over monitors. "Great job today, team. Bonus Friday after our win!" Lies, all of it. I packed slowly, eyes on the clock. One more night, then nine a.m. Felicity slipped me a note: Sisters in shit. Tomorrow we rise. Jasper fist-bumped me discreetly. Driving home, rage simmered into cold determination. Ragina's identity theft had backfired—my flag tipped authorities, Felicity's mess was another nail. The web closed, her empire of delusion crumbling.

At home, insomnia gripped me again. I paced, replaying the bank footage in my head, her smug face. My mental health frayed—therapy bills I'd pay from tainted savings? Anxiety spiked: what if she succeeds elsewhere? Trauma layered on—Kendrick's threats, her rages, now this violation. Morally gray heroism—enduring for the takedown. The group chat buzzed softly: Jasper's memes, Felicity's check-ins. Our bond, forged in fraud's fire, was unbreakable.

Saturday loomed, raid day. But tonight, reflection hit hard. From April hire to this—newbie thrill to battle-hardened whistleblower. Ragina's narcissism, gambling sprees masked as networking, subs stiffed like Lila Hargrove, all unraveled by our grit. Cold triumph mixed with dread. One more sleep, then cuffs. The gloomy building's last day for me. Justice, gritty and real, waited.

Word count aside, the weight lifted slightly. We'd survived cameras, swaps, thefts. Felicity's bankruptcy, my near-ruin—fuel for testimony. Profanity-laced resolve: Fuck you, Ragina. Enjoy your last lunch. Sleep came fitfully, dreams of hazel eyes in cuffs. Tomorrow, the end.

Amanda Ray

The Final Payroll

Saturday morning finally arrived, and the parking lot felt emptier than usual. Jasper, Felicity, and I pulled in together, our cars forming a tight cluster like we were bracing for a storm. The gloomy gray building stared back at us, its windows dark and uninviting. No one else had shown up yet, not even Kendrick or the operations guys. The office was strangely quiet as we stepped inside, the usual hum of phones and printers missing. My heart pounded with a mix of anticipation and dread. After yesterday's identity-theft bombshell, the rage still simmered inside me, mixed with the anxiety that had been my constant companion for months. We had fed the feds everything, but now it was 9:00 a.m., raid time, and nothing was happening.

We settled at our desks on the main floor, pretending to work. Felicity's sturdy frame hunched over her keyboard, her tight dark curls in that no-nonsense bun, deep brown eyes scanning emails with forced focus. Jasper slouched in his chair, lanky legs stretched out, his messy sandy hair falling into his eyes as he fiddled with a pen, cracking a weak joke under his breath. "If this goes south, at least we'll have stories for the grandkids. 'Grandma took down a fraud queen with spreadsheets.'" His half-grin didn't reach his blue eyes, the perpetual mischief dimmed by the tension. I nodded, forcing a smile, but my hands trembled on the mouse. The trauma from Ragina's schemes, the forged wires, the personal theft attempts, weighed heavy. My savings account was safe for now, but Felicity's bankruptcy lingered in my mind, her kids' future shattered by this monster's delusions.

That's when Ragina burst out of her office, a bottle of champagne in hand, her bottle-blonde hair teased high, designer suit straining at the seams. It was 9:00 a.m., and she was already celebrating, glass fizzing with bubbly. The gold jewelry jangled as she waved the bottle like a trophy. "Team! Family! Get in here!" Her voice was shrill, laced with that saccharine charm she turned on when she thought she had won. We exchanged glances and gathered in the main area, standing awkwardly as she popped the cork with a bang that echoed too loudly in the quiet space. Foam spilled over her manicured talons, and she laughed, pouring sloppy glasses for everyone. An unopened sealed envelope sat forgotten on her desk behind her, left by the auditor who had finished yesterday. She hadn't touched it, too busy with her victory lap.

"Listen up," Ragina said, raising her glass high, hazel eyes darting around with paranoid glee. "We've beaten the audit! Those bean counters thought they could come in here and tear us apart, but I protected you. My family. No one messes with RT Construction!" She thrust a glass into Jasper's hand, then Felicity's, ignoring their stiff postures. I took mine reluctantly, the champagne sloshing. She gulped hers down, smacking her lips. "By the end of the day, huge bonuses for everyone. We're talking real money, not that chump change. I've got it all handled. Wires incoming, loans approved. We're unstoppable!" Her voice rose to a boastful pitch, delusions spilling out as she paced, suit jacket flapping.

The office smelled of cheap bubbly and her heavy perfume, a toxic mix that turned my stomach.

I glanced at the clock on the wall. 9:10 a.m. Nothing. No sirens, no boots. The anxiety spiked, a cold sweat breaking on my neck. Had the DA backed out? Did Ragina's fake server swap fool them after all? My hands shook harder, gripping the glass so tightly I thought it might shatter. Felicity caught my eye, her stoic face cracking with worry, maternal instinct flashing as she mouthed, Steady. Jasper shifted, his freckled face paling, but he played it off with a thumbs-up. Ragina noticed my trembling and zeroed in, pointing a talon at me. "Emily! What's with the shakes? Too excited for your bonus? You should be! After all I've done for you, loyal girl." Her laugh was mocking, piercing. I forced the words out. "Yeah, just... thrilled, boss." Inside, panic roared. This is it? Our tips, the evidence, Felicity's bankruptcy docs—all for nothing? The morally gray weight crushed me; we'd endured her rages, the surveillance hell, cashing dirty checks, all for this moment that wasn't coming.

9:15 a.m. Still silence. Ragina rambled on, oblivious, refilling her glass. "See this envelope? Audit's sign-off. Victory! Now, back to work, but first—to family!" She clinked glasses sloppily with Jasper, who muttered, "Cheers," his voice tight. The trauma etched on our faces—my worry lines deeper, Felicity's eyes shadowed, Jasper's grin gone—didn't faze her. She was in her narcissistic bubble, convinced her empire stood tall. My mind raced to yesterday's bank call, her face on that footage, stealing my identity after months of forging our company's soul. Profanity burned in my throat: Fucking psycho, enjoy your last toast. But doubt crept in. What if Kendrick had warned her? What if the feds hesitated on the wire-fraud charges?

Then it started. Heavy boots thudded in the hallway outside, rhythmic and urgent, like a heartbeat accelerating. The front doors exploded inward with a crash, wood splintering. A swarm of FBI agents in tactical vests and local police flooded the main floor, guns drawn but low, voices barking. "FBI! Hands up! Everyone freeze!" Chaos erupted. Agents fanned out, securing the space. Ragina's champagne glass slipped from her fingers, shattering on the carpet, golden liquid pooling like spilled treasure. Her imposing 5'10" frame froze, then she whirled, ghostly white draining from her heavily made-up face. "What the—? This is a mistake! I'm Ragina Thomas! You can't—"

She lunged toward me, talon pointing wildly. "She did it! Emily! She stole the money! I have proof on the cameras! She's been sabotaging me for months!" Her scream was volcanic, profanities flying. "That traitorous bitch framed me! Check the footage—she's the thief!" The agents ignored her completely, two in FBI windbreakers striding past straight to her office. They kicked the door wider, seizing her computer, yanking cords, bagging hard drives. One agent glanced at the sealed auditor's envelope, slipping it into an evidence bag without a word. Ragina's eyes bulged, realization dawning. Her empire, built on fake wires and shell companies, crumbled in seconds.

We stood frozen, the staff watching in stunned silence. Felicity's hands clenched at her sides, quiet strength radiating as she stared down the woman who had trashed her credit. Jasper's eyes widened, a flicker of triumph breaking through his anxiety. I felt adrenaline surge, panic flipping to grim relief. The agents moved efficiently, one cuffing Ragina's wrists as she thrashed. "You assholes! Sexist pigs! This is my company!" Her voice cracked, paranoia fully unleashed. But they tuned her out, focus laser-sharp on the digital evidence—our tips, Henderson's real drive, the timestamped Vegas loans. Her accusations bounced off like rain on armor.

The quiet before had been eerie; now the office buzzed with radios crackling and agents directing. "Secure the suspect." "Bag those monitors." Ragina's face was a mask of horror, makeup cracking as sweat beaded. She twisted toward us one last time, hazel eyes wild. "You all knew! My family—betrayers!" But the agents hauled her back, her heels scraping the carpet stained with champagne. Felicity whispered, "Fuck her. It's over." Her voice, direct and profane, cut through my daze. Jasper let out a shaky laugh. "Holy shit, showtime." The gritty reality hit: white-collar crime exposed, no more moral tightrope. Yet anxiety lingered—what about our jobs, the fallout?

Agents fanned through desks, collecting files and laptops. One approached me gently. "Ms. Harris? We got it all. Thanks for the tips." Relief washed over me, but trauma's echo pulsed—months of anxiety, near-panic attacks in bathroom stalls, the mental-health toll of her delusions. Ragina's final betrayal, framing me on live TV, essentially, twisted the knife. She'd always played the victim, blaming us for her gambling sprees, her luxury lies. Now, ghostly pale, she was led toward the door, her empire in ruins.

The main floor emptied fast, neighbors peeking from across the lot as squad cars waited. We sank into chairs, breathing heavily. Silence fell again, heavier now with finality. Jasper cracked his knuckles. "Bonuses my ass. Real payday's justice." Felicity nodded, unclipping her bun, curls tumbling. "My kids get their mom back. No more forged shit." I stared at the champagne puddle, mind replaying the boots, the crash, her screams. Dark comedy flickered—champagne at 9 a.m. for her downfall toast—but grit dominated. We'd survived, bonded in this hell, morally gray heroes in a crime saga.

Outside, the gloomy building looked smaller, deflated. Police taped the doors, agents loading evidence vans. Ragina's Bentley sat abandoned, soon to be repossessed. My hands still shook, not from fear now, but release. The auditor's envelope had been the last nail; unopened, but its contents damning. We'd won, but the wreckage stared back—bounced dreams, stolen identities. Still, for the first time, hope edged in. The staff—our makeshift family—intact. Jasper fist-bumped me. "Told ya, dream team." Felicity smiled faintly, maternal warmth returning.

Hours blurred as statements were taken. An agent detailed the charges: wire fraud, money laundering, identity theft—hers and ours. "Her cloud storage? Goldmine. Your breadcrumbs sealed it." Profanity escaped me. "That fucking cunt tried to drain my savings yesterday." He nodded. "On record now. Whistleblower safe." Anxiety ebbed, trauma's grip loosening. We'd exposed the hollowness, rebuilt in the fire. Ragina's perceived victory, shattered mid-toast. Perfect.

By noon, the lot had cleared, but we lingered, processing. The quiet office felt haunted, desks littered with half-finished work. I thought of Lila Hargrove, the sub stiffed on payments; her ledgers were part of the case now. Kendrick's absence screamed—he'd probably flipped early. The morally gray threads untangled. Felicity hugged me. "Sisters through shit." Jasper grinned fully. "Coffee run? Real stuff, no bubbly." Laughter bubbled up, genuine. The raid's chaos faded, leaving gritty triumph. No more deranged boss, no more fear. Freedom tasted like champagne spilled on carpet— messy, golden, ours.

The Meltdown

The agents had Ragina by the arms now, her bottle-blonde hair whipping around as she twisted and kicked against their hold. Her designer heels scraped across the carpet, leaving scuff marks in the champagne stain that had spread like a bad omen. We watched from the main floor—me, Felicity, and Jasper rooted in place—the air thick with the crackle of radios and the sharp scent of spilled bubbly mixed with her heavy perfume. Outside, through the glass doors, squad cars lined the parking lot, their lights flashing silently in the morning sun. Neighbors from the strip mall across the way peeked from behind curtains, phones probably already out, capturing the show.

Ragina's piercing hazel eyes locked on me as they dragged her toward the exit. "You traitorous bitch!" she screamed, her voice shrill and breaking, echoing off the gloomy gray walls of the building. "I made your fucking career, Emily! You owe me everything! This is bullshit—you stole from me!" Spit flew from her lips, her gaudy gold jewelry jangling wildly with every thrash. The agents didn't flinch, one muttering into his vest mic, "Suspect resisting. Moving to transport." She turned her rage outward, spotting the neighbors gawking. "Fuck you all! Nosy pricks, filming my downfall? This is harassment!" Then to the cops: "Sexist pigs! You think you can cuff a woman like me? Call the governor!" Her imposing frame bucked, but they hauled her through the doors, her screams carrying into the lot like a siren.

Felicity crossed her arms over her sensible blouse, her deep brown eyes steady, that stoic powerhouse vibe holding firm. "Let the bitch howl," she said low, her Midwestern clip laced with profanity for emphasis. "She's done." Jasper let out a shaky breath beside me, his lanky frame slouched against a desk, messy sandy hair falling into his twinkling blue eyes. "Holy crap, that was Oscar-worthy. Think it'll go viral?" His half-grin flickered, masking the anxiety we'd all carried for months. I nodded, my heart hammering, but the panic from the raid's delay had flipped to something raw—relief edged with trauma. My hands still shook from the adrenaline, the mental weight of six months feeding evidence to the feds crashing down. We'd survived her delusions, the forged wires, the identity-theft attempts that nearly drained my savings. Morally gray? We'd walked that line, cashing dirty checks while plotting her fall.

In the parking lot, the scene unfolded like a gritty crime show, but all too real. Ragina's Bentley sat abandoned nearby, a fitting tombstone for her empire. Police taped off the building, evidence vans humming as agents loaded boxes of hard drives and files—the Lifeboat Ledger, her fake bank statements, shell-company docs. She kept screaming as they shoved her toward a cruiser, her power suit rumpled, makeup streaking like war paint. "Emily! You'll burn for this! My family betrays me? Fuck you!" One last glare over her shoulder, eyes wild with paranoia, before they ducked her head inside. The door slammed, muffling her to echoes. Neighbors whispered, one shouting, "About time, Ragina! You stiffed my brother on a job!" She banged on the window, but it was over. Cuffs glinted in the sun as the car pulled away.

Back inside, the office felt hollow, desks littered with half-empty coffee mugs and scattered papers. An agent in a windbreaker approached us, his face all business. "Staff? Company's going into receivership immediately. Court order. No access, no paychecks pending audit. You're out of jobs, but safe. Whistleblower protections apply—the FBI thanks you." He nodded at me specifically. "Your tips sealed it, Harris." Felicity exhaled hard, her practical watch ticking like a countdown to freedom. "Fuck yes. My kids won't eat forged promises anymore." Jasper fist-bumped the air. "Unemployed but alive? I'll take it." I sank into a chair, the weight hitting. No more RT Construction hell, no more Ragina's rages, but the wreckage stared back—resumes to dust off, references tainted by scandal.

Meanwhile, across town at the station, Ragina sat in the interrogation room, her voluminous hair deflated, suit jacket tossed aside. The lead investigator, a no-nonsense woman named Agent Reyes with a tight ponytail and sharp eyes, slid a folder across the metal table. "Ms. Thomas, let's cut the theatrics. We've got everything." Ragina sneered, wrists cuffed to the ring, talons tapping furiously. "This is a sexist hit job! The construction industry's boys' club hates a strong woman like me. I demand my lawyer! Call the governor—he owes me!" Her voice boomed off the cinderblock walls, but Reyes just flipped open the folder, revealing printouts of the Lifeboat Ledger—her secret tally of fake wires, gambling debts masked as "Vegas retreats," shell loans that funneled cash into designer sprees.

Ragina's hazel eyes darted, her facade cracking. "Fake! All fabricated by traitors!" Reyes tapped her tablet, queuing a video from Ragina's own cloud storage—grainy footage of her in a penthouse suite, manicured hands shoving chips across a blackjack table, laughing hysterically as thousands vanished. "Your 'networking retreats,' Ms. Thomas. Timestamped to the exact wires your staff flagged. Over two million in fraud. And this?" Another clip: Ragina at her desk late at night, forging my bank details, trying to siphon funds. Her face paled, sweat beading through heavy makeup. "That's... edited. From inside! One of my people betrayed me!"

Reyes leaned in, voice steady. "The evidence came from your house, your servers. Breadcrumbs from insiders. But you're right—someone flipped." Ragina lunged forward, chains rattling. "I'll give you Kendrick! That muscle-bound idiot handled the strong-arming, the vendor threats. He fudged site reports, extorted subs. Take him down, I'll testify!" Desperation cracked her voice, alternating with sobs. "I've sacrificed everything for RT! Bootstrapped from nothing, protected my family—my kids need me!" Tears smeared her mascara, her imposing build slumping. Reyes shook her head. "Blaise? He cut a deal three days ago. Full testimony, docs, everything. You're alone, Ragina."

The betrayal hit like a gut punch. Ragina wailed, her head dropping to the table. "That disloyal fuck! After all I did?" Her narcissistic bubble burst, paranoia proven self-fulfilling. Reyes stood. "Wire fraud, money laundering, identity theft—federal time. No governor's saving you." Ragina whimpered about sacrifices, then raged again.

"Sexist cunts! All of you!" But the door clicked shut, leaving her with the wreckage of her delusions.

Back at the lot, hours had passed. The sun beat down on the taped-off building, neighbors dispersed but gossip buzzing. Felicity had called her ex for kid pickup, her sturdy mom jeans dusty from pacing. Jasper scrolled his phone, memes flying in our group chat—dark comedy to cope. "Ragina's meltdown vid already at 500 views. Caption: 'When the champagne pops wrong.'" I wandered outside, my legs jelly, the adrenaline crash hitting hard. The curb felt like the only solid thing, so I sat, knees to chest, tears finally spilling. Months of anxiety, near-panic attacks in the bathroom, trauma from her screams, the forged loans that nearly bankrupted Felicity—it all poured out. We're free, but what now? Jobless, scarred, but alive. The morally gray haze lifted; we'd done right, exposed the white-collar rot.

Jasper plopped down beside me, handing over a steaming cup from the gas station across the street—real coffee, black and hot, no bubbly bullshit. "Hey, big sis. First real sip in months." His boyish freckles crinkled with a genuine grin, his lanky arm around my shoulders. Felicity joined us, cross-trainers crunching gravel, her quiet strength enveloping us. "Breathe, team. We're the survivors." No jokes now, just somber relief. The parking lot, once our daily dread, stretched empty, the gloomy gray building a relic. We'd pulled into it every day, friendship our anchor against Ragina's storms. Now we were out of jobs, but the noose was gone.

I sipped the coffee, the bitter warmth grounding me. "She called me a traitorous bitch. Said she made my career." Laughter bubbled up, gritty and real. Jasper snorted. "Career? More like a nervous-breakdown subscription. But yeah, we wrecked her empire." Felicity nodded, maternal edge softening. "Fuck her sacrifices. Mine kept me up nights, worrying about evictions for my kids. This? Justice." Her voice cracked, profanity underscoring the trauma we'd shared—profanity-laced group chats venting over her rages, anxiety spikes during fake billing marathons.

The lot quieted as the last agent van pulled away. Kendrick's truck was gone; his flip confirmed, another layer of her paranoia validated. Lila Hargrove's unpaid invoices, our tips—they'd built the case. Ragina's Vegas videos, her own cloud damning her high-roller facade. I wiped my tears, my chest loosening. "Receivership means no more RT, but no more fear." Jasper raised his energy drink. "To dream teams and downfall toasts." We clinked—coffee, soda, Felicity's water bottle—somber cheers amid wreckage.

Sitting there, the curb biting into my scuffed flats, I felt the mental-health toll recede. Trauma lingered, sure—anxiety would spike at loud voices for months—but we'd reclaimed something. Emily Harris, whistleblower, not victim. Jasper's prankster optimism, Felicity's unflappable grit—our bonds forged in fraud's fire. Ragina's screams echoed faintly in memory, her "family" speech a joke now. Dark comedy in her 9 a.m. champagne flop, gritty reality in the cuffs. White-collar crime unraveled, neighbors' stares turning into nods of respect.

As the sun dipped, casting long shadows over the lot, a receiver's truck arrived, signs posted: "Closed by Court

Order." We stood, hugging tight. "Dinner soon? Non-RT place," Jasper quipped. Felicity smiled. "Monthly check-ins. RT Trauma Support Group." I laughed, tears drying. Free, unemployed, but breathing. The chapter closed on her deranged reign, ours just beginning.

Amanda Ray

The Aftermath

Six months had passed since that chaotic day in the parking lot, and here I was, standing in the stark fluorescence of the federal courthouse. The air smelled of polished wood and stale coffee, a far cry from the gloomy gray building that had been our prison. My hands gripped the edge of the witness stand, knuckles white, as I faced the courtroom for the first time since the raid. Ragina Thomas sat at the defense table, a shadow of her former self. No more designer power suits straining at the seams, no voluminous bottle-blonde hair defying gravity. Instead, she wore a cheap orange jumpsuit that hung loose on her diminished frame, her hazel eyes dull and darting, heavy makeup replaced by the pallor of jail life. Her gaudy gold jewelry was gone, her manicured talons clipped short. She looked small, broken, like the empire she built on lies had finally crushed her.

The judge, a stern man with wire-rimmed glasses, cleared his throat and turned to me. "Ms. Harris, please state your full name and occupation for the record."

"Emily Harris," I said, my voice steady despite the knot in my stomach. "Former office manager at RT Construction. Now working at StableBuild Partners."

The prosecutor, a sharp woman in a navy suit, nodded encouragingly. "Ms. Harris, can you describe the fraudulent activities you witnessed under Ms. Thomas's direction?"

I took a breath, the words I'd rehearsed for months flowing out. "It started small, with lost clients blamed on us when it was her operations team—Jesse, William, and later Kendrick—dropping the ball. Then the pressure mounted. She demanded we bill everything, chase collections aggressively, but money was vanishing. We lost two major accounts in one week, and she screamed it was our fault. In her office, she ranted that we needed cash urgently. Turns out, it funded her vacations, her gambling sprees disguised as networking. She had us create fake wire transfers, backdate invoices, even take out loans she couldn't repay. Over two million dollars were stolen through shell companies and forged bank statements. She ruined dozens of lives—vendors unpaid, employees terrified, families on the brink."

Ragina's head snapped up, her voice shrill even from across the room. "Lies! That traitorous bitch is lying! I built that company from nothing!" The judge banged his gavel, warning her to be silent, but her eyes burned into me, that old paranoia flickering. I met her gaze, unflinching. This was the end, the justice we'd clawed for through six months of secret recordings, group-chat strategies, and near-panic attacks in the office bathroom.

The prosecutor presented the evidence: the Lifeboat Ledger printed in massive font on screens around the courtroom, videos from her own cloud storage showing her forging documents late at night, wire transfers timestamped to her Vegas benders. Victim testimonies rolled in—subcontractors stiffed on hundred-thousand-dollar jobs, employees with bounced paychecks, families facing eviction. Lila Hargrove took the stand before me, her short-cropped auburn hair neat, khakis crisp. "RT owed us $180,000 for excavation on three sites. Checks bounced, threats from her enforcer Kendrick. Emily's tips got us the proof to freeze assets. Saved my crew, my business." Ragina slumped, whispering to her lawyer, but the facade was gone.

The sentencing phase hit like a hammer. The judge reviewed the counts: wire fraud, money laundering, forgery, identity theft. "Ms. Thomas, your actions defrauded victims of over two million dollars, destroyed livelihoods, and eroded trust in an industry reliant on integrity. This court sentences you to fifteen years in federal prison, followed by five years of supervised release, and full restitution."

Fifteen years. The number hung in the air. Ragina wailed, collapsing onto her lawyer. "No! This is a sexist hit job! I sacrificed everything for my kids, my company!" But the gavel fell, final, bailiffs hauling her away. She shot me one last venomous look, diminished and defeated. I stepped down, legs shaky, the weight of my testimony lifting like fog burning off in sunlight.

In the hallway outside the courtroom, the crowd thinned, footsteps echoing on marble. Lila Hargrove approached, her sturdy build moving with purpose, faded tattoos peeking from rolled sleeves. She extended a callused hand. "Emily, I owe you everything. That evidence you slipped to the feds? It froze her accounts before she could drain the last of our payments. My business is back on track—paid the crew, kept the equipment loans current. Hell, we're bidding on new projects. You didn't just take her down; you saved folks like me from going under."

I shook her hand, a genuine smile breaking through. "We all did it together, Lila. Your ledgers were key. No more shell games."

She nodded, hazel eyes sharp behind glasses. "Time to put the hammer down for good. Thanks again." She walked off, shoulders squared, a survivor like us.

Six months earlier, we'd been jobless, sitting on that curb with real coffee, the wreckage of RT Construction taped off. Now, life had pieced itself back together, stronger. Felicity, Jasper, and I had landed on our feet. Felicity's stoic efficiency shone in her new admin role at a logistics firm, her kids' college funds secure, no more nights worrying about eviction. "I've got two little ones counting on stability," she'd text in our group chat. "Fuck if I'll let another Ragina near us." Jasper, the lanky jokester, parlayed his quick numbers into a project-coordinator gig at a union contractor, his dad jokes now lightening board meetings instead of defusing rages. "From fraud memes to real paychecks—upgrade complete 😂," his texts read.

Me? StableBuild Partners was a dream. Sensible blouses, scuffed flats traded for comfortable loafers, a boss who knew my name for spotting efficiencies, not forging wires. Checks cleared on time, every time. The office buzzed with actual teamwork, no screams echoing down hallways. My chestnut bob stayed neat, worry lines fading from my forehead. But trauma lingered, a gritty undercurrent. Loud voices still spiked my anxiety—a manager's raised tone in a meeting sent my heart racing, palms sweating, flashbacks to Ragina hurling staplers. Breathe, Emily, I'd think. She's gone. Fifteen years gone. Therapy helped, unpacking the morally gray months of cashing dirty money while plotting her fall. The anxiety ebbed, slower some days, but it was progress.

We met for dinner once a month, our RT Trauma Support Group, at a cozy Italian place downtown. No gloomy gray building, no parking-lot dread. Tonight, under warm pendant lights, plates of pasta steaming, we clinked glasses of red wine. Felicity arrived first, tight dark curls in a neat bun, deep brown eyes bright. Her gold wedding band glinted as she hugged me. "Kids are thriving—soccer, straight A's. No more bounced-check nightmares."

Jasper slid into the booth next, messy sandy hair tamed, freckled grin wide. "New gig's gold. Boss actually laughs at my jokes. No Kendrick breathing down my neck." He pulled up his phone, showing a meme: Ragina in cuffs captioned, "When the empire flops." We laughed, dark comedy still our balm.

"To new beginnings," I toasted, my voice warm. "And never hearing 'Do you know who I am?' again."

Felicity raised her glass, maternal edge soft. "Fuck that noise. We're the dream team that outlasted the deranged one. My anxiety's down—sleeping through the night now."

"Same," Jasper added. "Therapy's weird, but unpacking the trauma? Worth it. Thought my humor was just hiding shit, but nah, it's my superpower."

We shared stories, the gritty reality of recovery. Felicity confessed panic over job applications, fearing scandal-taint. Jasper admitted nightmares of Ragina's screams. I opened up about my triggers. "Heard a loud voice in the hall last week—froze, heart pounding. But I breathed through it. Getting better." Profanity slipped in naturally, emphasis on the wins. "That bitch thought she owned us. Fifteen years says otherwise." Bonds forged in fraud's fire held strong, monthly check-ins our anchor.

Later, driving home to my stable apartment—rent paid, no loan sharks lurking—I glanced at photos on the dashboard. My kids, finally settled after the chaos. Mom had taken them in during the worst of it, but now they had a real home, laughter filling rooms instead of tension. Soccer practices, bedtime stories, no shadows of eviction. I pulled into the driveway, the normalcy a gift. I did the right thing, I thought, my chest loosening. Exposed the white-collar rot, protected them from the ripple effects. Morally gray no more—justice over silence.

Inside, with the kids asleep, I booted up my laptop at the kitchen table. The secret drive hummed, the last remnant of the nightmare. Files: recordings, screenshots, the final Lifeboat Ledger backup. My finger hovered over Delete. Ragina's voice echoed in memory—"You traitorous bitch!"—but powerless now. Fifteen years. Vendors paid. Businesses saved. Us, thriving.

I hit Delete. One by one, the files vanished. The drive wiped clean. No more hidden folders, no more looking over my shoulder. I closed the laptop, a deep breath escaping. My voice, once muted in fear, now testified in courtrooms and at dinners alike. Life reclaimed, the deranged boss a closed chapter forever.

RT Construction was a ghost, receivership dissolving the husk. Kendrick rotted on a lesser sentence, his flip buying leniency. Ragina's kids faced their own reckonings, her "sacrifices" exposed as lies. Lila's firm expanded, a testament to pushback. Our group chat pinged—a Jasper meme, Felicity's thumbs-up. Laughter bubbled up, real and free.

I poured a nightcap, staring out at the quiet street. No squad cars, no screams. The tension was gone, gritty scars fading into strength. The mystery unraveled, the crime punished, the nonfiction hell turned triumph. We'd survived, bonded, rebuilt. Emily Harris, whistleblower, mother, friend. The end.

But wait, not quite. One last group text: "Next dinner? RT Trauma free forever." Replies flooded in: "Hell yes." "Abso-fucking-lutely." "Count me in."

I smiled, set the phone down. Forward, always forward.

Acknowledgements

Writing this book was its own kind of workplace survival story — and it would not exist without the people who kept me sane along the way.

To everyone who has ever sat in a toxic office, watched something wrong unfold in front of them, and had to decide what to do about it — this book is yours. Your resilience was the spark.

To my early readers, thank you for your honesty, your encouragement, and your willingness to read about Ragina Thomas without needing therapy afterwards. You are braver than you know.

To my editor, for seeing what this story could be and pushing it there.

And to anyone who has ever had to say the words "the cheque is in the mail" when they knew it absolutely was not — I see you.

Amanda Ray

About the Author

Amanda Ray writes fiction about the world of work — the absurdities, the power games, the small acts of courage that happen in ordinary offices every day. My Deranged Boss is her debut novel.